Flora McIvor

DONALD SMITH

Luath Press Limited

EDINBURGH

www.luath.co.uk

First published 2017

ISBN: 978-1910745-90-8

The author's right to be identified as author of this book
under the Copyright, Designs and Patents Act 1988 has been asserted.

The paper used in this book is recyclable.

Printed and bound by
Bell & Bain Ltd, Glasgow

Typeset in 11 point Sabon

For Naomi Mitchison

On the Feast Day of Bride
The Daughter of Ivor
Shall come from her mound
In the rocks amongst the heather.
I will not touch Ivor's daughter
Nor shall she harm me.

Alles ist ein Traum

A Note for Readers: Jacobites in Books

WHY DID SO many people in Scotland support the restoration of their exiled Stuart kings, not least in 1745 when it seemed a long shot?

In his first novel Waverley, Walter Scott provides an answer that most people still accept. It was a Romantic cause – a gallant adventure – though doomed to failure because it ignored the power of the British state, following the Union of England and Scotland in 1707. The main purpose of that Union had been to keep the exiled Stuarts out.

So Scott's treatment of his Jacobites in Waverley is admiring but also ironic – they will become mature adults in due course. That is why Flora McIvor, who is shaping up to be his heroine, must be sent to a nunnery, and the pallid hero Edward Waverley steered into the safer, more docile embrace of Rose Bradwardine. It is possible though to imagine a different future for Flora, one that reflects the powerful family loyalties and cultural values which motivated the Jacobites.

Which takes us to Alister Ruadh McDonell, often known as Young Glengarry since his father was chief of the Glengarry McDonells. They were among the most loyal of loyal Jacobite clans, and Alister Ruadh was pivotal in continuing Highland resistance after the defeat of the 1745 Rising at Culloden. The McDonells were later fêted by Walter Scott as the epitome of Highland virtues, which were happily harnessed to extending the British Empire through war and conquest. The Glengarry of his day gratefully presented Sir Walter with a pet deerhound.

But, unknown to Scott, and to subsequent readers, Young Glengarry had lived a double life. This left little trace, though perhaps it is no coincidence that Glengarry was the location of the first large scale clearance of Highlanders from their ancestral lands. I am grateful to Andrew Lang, a fellow writer and lover of Scotland, for painstakingly tracking down whatever documentary evidence my story can claim.

Overture

SHE WAS ON Clementina's right, set slightly back. Yet although she kept her shoulders rigid, she could by straining forward peer down into the theatre. She was drawn by its warmth, away from a cold draught that blew from the rear of the box and touched her upper back with goose pimples.

For a moment Flora felt that draught as a welcome relief. Her whole frame was burning, but the pictures in her mind were as vivid as the stage she saw below her. Candles flickered unevenly amidst a fug of velvets and satins. The gloom was lit by gleams of jewellery or glittering brocade.

She saw her thirteen year old self at a distance but clearly, as if through a spy glass. Then she heard the music. It seemed to come from the ferment inside her body. Somewhere in the dark recess of the pit, the overture had begun. The music was sombre but flowing and Flora felt her body relax as the melody sounded through and around. She had felt the same way in church as a girl when the choir filled the cavernous spaces, and she became part of the rising wave.

But Flora was not then free to dream. To the left Her Majesty was upright, unbending. The high narrow forehead was averted in denial of such worldly pleasure.

Her attendance was a duty – to be seen in the face of the world as consort of the legitimate king of Britain. The tiara glinting above her bound curls was worn like a crown of thorns. Queen Clementina's gaze was directed to her left on the two princes, her sons. Charles Edward and little Henry sat right against the balcony on the stage side to get the best view. Oblivious to their mother's determination that they be seen and admired, the boys were caught up in the music. Both were natural musicians, and for all her austerity Clementina was an indulgent mother, especially when it came to Charles Edward.

Calmed by the music, Flora's mind was back in those interminable days of shadowy waiting. Charles' cello had been a welcome diversion in the sombre routine favoured by Clementina. Her Majesty and His Majesty, King James, did not appear as a couple in Rome or travel together in public. It was as if there were two Courts at the Palazzo Muti existing side by side, between which the young princes were sole emissaries.

Flora focused on the memories in her mind, blocking out the twisted blankets, the narrow bed and the pain that demanded her attention.

What had she felt in the midst of those strange separations? Or had it not seemed strange? Her own parents were gone, and she had been taken away from her brother, who had stayed in France to be a soldier. The music had always been unalloyed pleasure; daily tension eased away.

King Orpheus and Eurydice his queen were singing together, blissfully carefree and in love, despite their royal alliance.

Welcome, my lord and love, Sir Orpheus,
In this life you ever are my king.

Each sang to the other and then the two voices intertwined and blended, till finally their lips met in a loving kiss, only for the music to swell once more, and for the voices to separate and join in gradual crescendo.

Faces of Flora's own long lost father and mother rose up in the darkness, like the miniature portraits she kept always at her bedside. They had loved each other as deeply as Orpheus and Eurydice, and had been divided by death. Yet she felt them still as loving presences, near to her in the same way that she and Fergus had been close, even though they too were kept apart. She wanted to enjoy the happiness of the lovers before they were sundered.

What if her own Lorenzo would not return? She would be left now in these rooms entombed by fire and pain forever. She reached out a hand from the covers but touched no-one. He too was lost. Even Bessie had gone.

She forced herself back to the candlelit stage. The underlying mood was brooding, but ornamented with forced happiness as Eurydice appeared. Soon tragic events were unfolding with the venomous sting of a snake prompting the removal of the young queen into the kingdom of death. Orpheus was left bereft as the music moved from disaster to lament. He could not stay in the palace alone, but taking his harp set out in search of his lost love. The scene was transformed by a backcloth of lonely woods, where he sat down on a rock and began to sing.

Flora saw immediately that the singer was not playing his harp, but drawing a demonstrative hand across its silent strings while the orchestra took up his plangent lament.

O doleful harp, with many a string,
Turn all thy mirth and music into mourning
And cease from all thy sweet melodies
To weep with me thy lord and king,

For I have lost in earth all my Joy –
Where hast thou gone my Eurydice?

Flutes became birds singing in sad harmony, while the
strings trembled like leaves in sympathy. This was how
she and Fergus had been left, when first their father and
then their mother had died in France. She no longer gazed
at the singer with his gold painted face and high-crested
wig. Instead she saw white skin and dark hair, and felt
the warm hand of her brother as he led his little sister
through the gardens at St Germain, pointing out her
favourite flowers. As Flora wandered in her memories,
Orpheus rose from his rock and continued to search,
begging the gods to aid his quest. Till suddenly a triple
masked monster burst from the wings – Cerberus, the
dread porter, guardian of hell's gate.

But Orpheus took up his harp again and lulled the
three heads to sleep. Something menacing entered the
music, as a procession of underworld beings came on
stage encircling Orpheus in a slow dance. They touched
him with black wands and nodding, dark plumed helmets
while he stood bewildered by this phantasmagoria, until
the dancers broke away on either side to reveal Hades
and Persephone raised on two thrones, etched in ebony
and silver. The audience gasped at the skill with which
this tableau had been revealed by the swift movement of
curtains behind the dancers. The king and queen of Death
wore half masks, which gave their faces a sinister cast,
and high pointed black crowns, studded with pearls.

Flora knew she had to tear off those masks. Who
was hidden there? Face after face was exposed in rapid
succession – James, Charles Edward, Murray, O'Kelly,
yet she also knew they were all disguises. Only one face
would appear, in its arrogant beauty, its cold disdain. She

struggled to get up but her body was weighted, enveloped. Strong hands were pressing her down. All she could do was watch, trapped in the royal box.

Orpheus went down on one knee, resting his harp on the other, and began to play. This music pled his sorrow and his desire. Persephone turned towards her lord, but he listened impassively until the music faded to its end, when he lifted his right hand and gestured towards the wings.

Unnoticed as the music played, Eurydice had stepped into the shadows. She was clothed in a plain white shift, and her face was deathly white, her hair cropped short, while her arms hung down helplessly on each side of her emaciated, fevered body. Orpheus moved instinctively in her direction, but then froze in shock as Eurydice came into the light. His anguish was barely audible.

My lovely lady, my delight,
How are you changed, how –
Where are your rosy cheeks,
Your crystal eyes and lashes dark,
Your lips so red, soft to kiss?

Persephone put a hand on Hades' arm, speaking in a full contralto.

Lord Hades, king of all below,
Recall my coming here to dwell,
My wasting and decline,
My mother's grief and woe,
Till your heart gave way
Yielding the boon of my return.

It seemed at first as if Hades would not even acknowledge this plea, staring inflexibly ahead through the eye slits of his mask. But then the orchestra took up compassion's cause.

Clementina Sobieski rose abruptly from her seat, turning her back on the stage, and moved stiffly towards the door at the rear. Charles Edward looked round crossly,

'Maman,' he hissed, 'you can't leave now.'

'Stay with Henry,' she instructed over her shoulder, 'I will send the carriage back before the final curtain.'

Flora should go with her mistress. Charles Edward looked back towards the action, the scene was dissolving, and Clementina was not to be seen. She tried to follow, but could not rise from this bed.

'Please, Missis, drink this, Master will be coming home soon. Drink this, Missis, so's you can lay back an' rest.'

I

AS FLORA CAME out of sleep, sunlight was filling her room. It flowed in waves through the narrow windows and the door onto the rampart which she had insisted on leaving unscreened. There was blue sky and a few puffy white clouds blowing in early spring air.

She was home, her own grown up self. It was true.

Just for a moment Flora stayed beneath warm blankets hugging the pleasure to herself.

Sounds were gradually filtering through. The talk of people below; the clash of bowls and platters as remnants of the night's feasting were cleared away; voices outside as the first clansmen of the day arrived or departed; the wheeling cries of birds that Flora was only beginning to be able to name and distinguish. How odd that all this should be fresh, when it was so old to her parents, like a birthright. To experience this after the seclusions of childhood, the gloomy curtained rooms, and the candlelit shadows. It was a world begun anew, her world.

Soon old Mairi would bring water in a cracked pitcher that had once belonged to Flora's grandmother. Nicolette, the maid she had brought with her from St Germain, as instructed by Fergus, would also be in attendance. But Nicolette was struggling in the absence of toilette, with the mealtimes when knives and fingers were the only implements, and the sight of bare hairy legs. She did not seem to be acquiring Flora's innate sense of ancient culture that lay beneath every aspect of Highland life.

Fergus, himself chief of Clan McIvor, was fully in command, having returned from exile two years before when the forfeitures of 1715 faded from the statutes. Flora's new role was to act the hostess for her unmarried brother. Clan envoys and messengers were arriving daily from all points of the compass. Things were stirring which was why Fergus had called his sister home. The opportunity to restore McIvor fortunes was looming.

Yet Flora's joys were the hunt and the poetry. She loved the feel of wind and rain on her face, out on the hill scenting deer to track. This was man's preserve yet as daughter and brother of a chief she claimed her rightful place at the hunt. Flora could put a musket to her shoulder as firmly as any gillie, and she could draw a bowstring and let fly swift and sure as any clansman. Only decorum prevented her racing to the kill and gralloching the fallen beast with her own dirk. Such physical freedom attacked every sense in her body like the shock of the clear cold air on long muffled skin.

But her deepest pleasure was in the poetry and music, the bardachd of the clan. Flora had never lost the childhood Gaelic that had surrounded her French infancy, though the idiom of Clan McIvor's Bard was rich and strange. Flora was determined to master this ancient tradition and to accompany her own halting Gaelic with the clarsach. This tree of strings seemed to resonate with the windblown hill country, the melancholy of its loves, and more recent struggles. This was her own culture, however distant and long denied. Like someone emotionally starving from a dragged out confinement, she wanted to grasp every impression, every experience, with both hands outstretched.

Suddenly, Mairi's wheezes could be heard on the twisting stair, and without a moment's further thought Flora swung out of her covers ready to splash the barely warm water generously over her tingling arms, shoulders and breasts. The sun embraced her white flesh as if she were a shining maiden of the dawn, while the old woman rubbed, and mopped and muttered in Gaelic around this long lost daughter of Ivor, who had at last come home.

Ablutions done, Flora pulled on her cotton petticoats and then the silk gown. Nicolette stood hapless while Flora added a tartan philabeg wrapped round twice like some eastern mantle. Then she was out on the ramparts, leaving Mairi's grumbles and her maid's tut-tutting adrift. With eyes closed she drew a deep lungful of bright air and, releasing it slowly into the breeze, she allowed her eyes to open onto a prospect she was sure she had once dreamed; if she was not dreaming still.

The brightness of morning was bringing out subdued colours from a landscape that had not yet fully woken to spring. The hill grasses were a dull yellow, the heather scrubbed by frost, and the birches huddled around the river leafless though silver in the sun. But those details were swept up by the scale of blue sky travelling over windblown clouds. They were like runners traversing the glens with feet barely touching the wintered earth.

The valley was unusually wide. Now that Flora had walked or ridden over most of the surrounding landscape, she realised that this glen was like a plateau. Below were much steeper valleys and narrow inclines twisting down towards the eastern lowlands. The river went directly south eventually reaching a steep, rocky pass which guarded by the castle of Baron Bradwardine, the McIvor's longstanding friend and neighbour. Once this had been a hostile gateway; dividing Highland and Lowland.

To the north, the wide glen was populated with scattered townships of single-roomed stone cottages. In them, family and animals shared the smoke filled, earth floored accommodation all winter. Beyond were the summer huts or sheilings, to which the cattle were driven leaving the lower ground for corn and oats. Further again, much higher mountains raised sharp peaks still streaked with snow. On some days when Flora looked from her tower those peaks seemed far distant, but on others when the air was still or moist they seemed to be unexpectedly clear, and near at hand.

But Flora's gaze was more focused on what was happening around the castle. This was the McIvor realm though the stronghold was a tower house more than a castle. It had been built by Fergus' grandfather who had decided to make this his ancestral seat, so bringing the former wanderings of the Clan Ivor to an end. Or so he had hoped. The ground spread out in all directions except east where a series of rocky ledges protected the flank of the rude fortress.

So extended was the valley that below the castle the river flowed into a broad shallow loch, and then out again at its southern end into the narrow descent. The loch, nearly two miles in length, was a moat for the kingdom of McIvor, and a ready source of fish and game birds for the hard pressed, hospitable chiefs. There were several islands in the loch and its edges were fringed with woodland, indented bays and a few pebbled beaches. Small boats were already on the water, one under sail.

Below the tower itself the ground levelled out towards the loch providing a natural gathering place for games or parades but there was no garden, formal or informal. Fergus' piper was already tuning up for his morning salute and, as Flora had heard from her room at the top of the castle, a bustle of arriving and departing messengers fanned out from the gateway. She tore herself reluctantly away from the view to get the day's news.

When Flora came down into the hall a table was already set out at the upper end with bowls of porridge and, in concession to foreign ways, some bread made from fine milled flour. The normal supplies of small ale and usquebagh were to hand, but beside them sat a solitary china tea cup waiting for infusion of the luxury leaves. So much as usual, but where was Fergus? Suddenly he hurried in already booted, and with his philabeg wrapped tight for travel.

'Forgive me, Flora, but I must go to meet an unexpected guest.'

'Who is that?'

'Captain Waverley of Waverley Honour.'

'An English officer is our guest?'

'He comes from an old Jacobite family, and he is staying with the good Baron at Tullyveolan.'

'I thought you were in dispute with Baron Bradwardine.'

'A mere trifle of missing cattle. That misunderstanding has been washed away by our retrieval of beasts lifted by Donald Lean. Evan Dhu has been about the business.'

'Donald Lean is a rogue, and I don't know why you indulge him,' chided Flora, galled to think how McIvor's association with that lawless cateran must look in the eyes of the Baron and his gently educated daughter, Rose.

'Even rogues have their uses.' The lines round Fergus' dark McIvor eyes crinkled in a smile which his mouth refused. 'It is Donald that has brought Edward Waverley to Castle McIvor at this moment.'

'Is he a serving officer?'

'His regiment is stationed at Dundee. But we need the Jacobite English above all men.'

'Would Waverley of Waverley Honour desert his commission?'

'He is on leave visiting the Baron. Their families, as you know, served together in the Rising of 1715. We cannot ask anything dishonourable of our guest, but when the time comes for action... We must test his intentions, and encourage a change of heart.'

'Are things really at a crisis, Fergus?' Flora had taken hold of her brother's arm and pulled him a little towards her.

The McIvor eyes swivelled out of focus. His face became blank, smooth skinned. 'I must go or we will be late. Come, Calum,' he shouted over Flora's shoulder, 'we'll go and meet Euan Dhu on the way.'

The figure sweeping from the hall, followed by his personal attendant, was compact and sturdy; he seemed to take all the energy with him out of the room. His less than average height was balanced by broad shoulders, controlled force and poise. Though traditionally equipped with sword, pistols and dirk, Fergus wore tartan trews and sported a stylish bonnet with three eagle feathers. His dark beard was closely trimmed with the rest of his tanned face shaven and shining.

Flora dipped some bread in cream and slowly scooped up porridge from a wooden bowl. After chewing a few mouthfuls she retired back to her chamber on the topmost storey to reconsider the dressing of her own unruly raven hair.

Later in the morning, in accordance with the routine of recent months, MacMurrough the Bard appeared to give Flora instruction in the music of the clarsach. Using a combination of her childhood Gaelic, the clan poet's elementary English, and the universal language of music, steady progress was being made. Yet Flora's attention was not on the old man's lessons.

'We are expecting a guest.'

'An English.'

'Yes, but not any Englishman. Captain Waverley is a soldier of ancient family, loyal to our king.'

'The king over the water!' MacMurrough looked round for a flask from which he could pledge his loyalty. 'We are in strange times to be welcoming a redcoat.'

'Perhaps, you will compose a poem for the occasion?' Flora was unsure of the etiquette, yet knew that the Bard could compose spontaneously when he chose.

'The Bard will sing in honour of his chief.'

'Of course,' Flora acquiesced, 'yet the chief's guests are also deserving of honour.'

MacMurrough began to stroke the strings and to recite some classic verses about the beauty, strength, fame, endurance, audacity, wisdom and virtue of Fergus McIvor, culminating with his generosity to poets and harpers. As Flora murmured appreciation the Bard began a catalogue of all the Highland clans and their qualities. Flora was barely able to follow but understood that the selection of MacDonalds, McDonells, MacLeans, Camerons and MacNeills, amongst others, was based on their allegiance to the exiled Stuarts.

Then came an unfamiliar verse that Flora made MacMurrough repeat until she had the sense and the melody at her own command.

Fair-haired stranger from the land that is green
Whose steed is shining and smooth as raven's wing
And raises its head to neigh like the eagle's battle cry,
Remember the faith and courage of your forbears,
The loyalty they held in their hearts without faltering.

Clearly, Fergus had already briefed the Bard as to what might be required, and Flora was happy to follow suit, till she had the song fully learned.

After MacMurough's withdrawal, Flora called Nicolette, to wash her hair and curl its tumbling waves into more orderly ringlets. This evening had turned into a test for the young McIvors, who had been left orphans and exiles to pick up the ragged threads of their heritage. Flora was determined to succeed whatever the cost to herself. Even the small pension she received from the will of Clementina Sobieski, her deceased royal mistress, had been diverted to the support of the clan's officers, not least the Bard and his extended family. When her hair was dried, Flora had her best silks laid out on the bed. Despite several variations of ribbon and lace, pride of place remained with the McIvor plaid wrapped round her bare white shoulders. The combination even viewed in her mottled mirror was striking.

By late afternoon Flora was out on the battlements which were still warmed by sunlight coming from the western side of the glen. There were a few boats still on the loch but the main activity was on the other side of Castle McIvor. In the distance, straggles of people could be seen moving out of the townships. Closer to hand these appeared as family groups heading towards the evening gathering. Below the walls, clansmen were milling about in their best philabegs, fully armed with claymores, pistols, dirks and metal studded shields slung over their shoulders. At their centre a smaller group – the chief's personal bodyguard – held Lochaber axes in addition to their other weapons. There was no sign of Fergus.

Suddenly the sound of bagpipes was heard from the lochside. One of the boats had pushed ashore and Flora could see three figures stepping out. First unmistakably came the tall frame of Evan Dhu, then Fergus, and lastly, helped out by Evan, a slender red-coated stranger. The three began to walk towards the castle, gathering an escort as they came.

Meanwhile the bustle below had formed itself into an assembly. The men stood in curved rows fanning out from the gateway, each rank bristling with weapons. As the three figures came closer there was a strange groaning as more bagpipes were swelled, and a wave of sound broke into the air. When the chief himself appeared the men clashed swords on shields and shouted in acclamation. Fergus stopped with the redcoat at his side and Evan behind. He raised his hand and silence fell.

'The McIvor is honoured by the greeting of his people. And our clan is honoured to welcome Edward Waverley. You must excuse our customs, Captain Waverley. I had forgotten that some of my clansmen were gathering today for our feast.'

At a signal from Evan, the clashing of swords and skirling of pipes broke out again. Listening now from the shelter of her room, Flora could imagine the tall fair-haired stranger being ushered through the battered gates, as if this display of martial tradition was a routine hardly worth particular notice. As yet, Flora herself had been unable to get a good look at the young man whom Fergus was so determined to impress.

By the time Flora was summoned to the high table of the feast everyone was in their places. As she approached, Captain Waverley rose to his feet and she nodded in acknowledgement of his courtesy but slipped past unnoticed to her seat on Fergus' left hand. The din was deafening and ruled out polite conversation.

The chief and his principal guests sat at an extended

top section of a huge oak table which stretched the length of the hall which in turn took up the whole ground floor of the castle. Below Fergus, Waverley and visitors from neighbouring clans were Clan McIvor's main land holders, most of whom were related through ties of blood or ancient obligation to the chief. Next were the officers of the chief's household and below them again the clansmen, small farmers and cottars who made up the body of the clan. On this occasion the feast continued on trestles out the hall doors into the courtyard and then onto the green beyond. The lower tables were surrounded by landless men, dependents, women, children and finally a tumultuous host of dogs which having come in various company were now vying lustily for place and attention.

Men and women moved busily about the tables bringing food, replenishing drinking vessels and scooping up leftovers to carry down to the dogs and humans, who were below even the lowest table. Those at the high end were eating from boards and ashets piled with finely dressed cuts of venison, mountain hare, whole salmon, grouse and ptarmigan. Further down the table were roughly hewn joints of mutton and beef, but the centrepiece was a whole roast lamb still standing upright with a sprig of parsley stuck in its mouth. Those nearby hacked at the carcass with their dirks.

Further down again were pots of broth, cheese, onions and oatcakes, supplemented by the leftovers from higher up. These supplies were constantly passed on to the crowd outside. Drinks were administered in the same degree with champagne and claret flowing at the top end while whisky and then strong beer were poured as the table descended. At the far end penny ale found its way in copious quantities through the hall doors so ensuring that none felt slighted or excluded.

Since her own arrival some months before, Flora had experienced many clan feasts but there was something hectic and raucous about this occasion. There were more armed clansmen gathered than she had seen before; barely suppressed excitement and even fervour seemed to possess the whole company. Flora wondered what Captain Waverley of Waverley Honour would make of such an excess of Highland custom. It was certainly too noisy to ask, as neighbours competed to be heard across a table that looked increasingly like the aftermath of a battle.

Then suddenly the hubbub subsided. Bidden or unbidden, MacMurrough had taken up his place beside the fire. He stood small harp in hand, as the last voices died away, and when the Bard was satisfied he had the assembly's full attention he struck his first chord. Flora knew what was coming and followed closely. First was the traditional panegyric of the chief, his ancestry, valour and virtue, the strength of his fighting men, the loyalty of his whole clan to their last breath. Next came praise of neighbouring and allied clans, at which their representatives at the high table rose and bowed in gracious recognition. Then came the verse praising Waverley. Flora stole a glance in his direction as did many others in the hall. The young visitor remained still and formally upright, though clearly gripped by this unfamiliar performance.

Then abruptly the music changed to a more vigorous tempo. MacMurrough struck the strings with renewed force and poured a passionate river of angry words into the atmosphere. This was unexpected but Flora recognised the form if not the precise meaning. This was a call to arms and incitement to battle. She could feel the pent up energy build till it could be held back no longer and with a full throated roar the long table took up the refrain, fists, knives and gun butts beating on the oak boards.

MacMurrough let it play out, and then as adroitly pulled back the volume and pace, and the company subsided with him. As the Bard let the last chords fall into silent place he turned and bowed deeply towards his chief. In reply Fergus rose to his feet and raised a delicately chiselled silver cup to the Bard before draining it in one quaff. Then he passed the cup to an attendant who took it in gift to MacMurrough. At this the whole crowd burst out once again in cheering and applause. The poet raised his cup in triumph.

As MacMurrough stepped away from the cavernous stone fireplace a piper struck up. Flora knew this was the signal for redoubled drinking that would go on through the rest of the evening. It was time for her to retreat and prepare to receive Waverley in her withdrawing room on the top floor of the old tower.

'This is my sister's kingdom, Captain Waverley. My writ does not run here, since she is as much a power in Clan McIvor. For our people tradition is everything, and Flora has drunk more deeply at that stream.'

'That is exactly what interests me,' replied a cultured, pleasantly modulated voice, 'the civilisation of your Highland nation.'

'Well, you will find satisfaction here then, despite the steep ascent. I am a mere soldier, weighed down by practical affairs.'

Flora could hear this exchange as the voices came up the last steps and through her door. The room they entered was spartan by Waverley's standards, and even by those of the Palazzo Muti, yet good taste was on display wherever you looked. Two high backed carved chairs sat either side of a modest fireplace. Old French tapestries softened bare stone walls, and in the middle of the room a small circular table of polished wood set off some Venetian glass which glowed in the light of the fire. Against the south wall, beneath a narrow window slit, was an escritoire on top of which was ranged a row of leather bound literary volumes, French, English and Italian. Some small devotional books were laid on the desk top.

There was a recess on the north side in which Nicolette sat demurely on a low stool. But the centrepiece of the chamber was its mistress who sat on the fire's right hand, upright and elegant. Flora's resemblance to her brother was immediately apparent, but whereas he breathed vigour and repressed energy her face appeared fragile in repose like fine white porcelain. The intense pallor of her skin set off the dark eyes and black hair tumbling down her neck. Yet Flora's delicate frame sat firmly in the cradle of the chair, possessed by its own strength of resolve.

'My dear Flora, here is Captain Waverley to make your acquaintance. I must tell you, before I return to the barbarous rituals of our forefathers, that young Waverley is a worshipper of the Celtic muse, as of tonight – not least because he does not understand a word of Gaelic. I have assured him that you are eminent as a translator of Highland poetry and that MacMurrough highly esteems your versions of his bardachd, on the same principle as Waverley admires the originals, namely he doesn't understand the language. Please have the goodness to recite to our guest the string of names MacMurrough tacked together this evening. I am sure you have a version since you are in the Bard's councils and know every new song before he rehearses them in the hall.'

Waverley seemed to stoop slightly in embarrassment without in any way denying his enthusiasm.

'Fergus, how can these verses possibly interest an English stranger? Even if I could translate them as you claim.'

'They have interest enough for me,' complained the chief, 'since they've cost me the last of my silver cups.'

'When the hand of the chief is closed, the breath of the Bard is frozen,' Flora quoted.

'Quite so, and God knows what I can give him next time the Muse has a thaw. There are three things useless for today's Highlander – a sword he cannot draw, a Bard to sing of deeds he dare not emulate, and a goatskin sporran that lacks a single golden guinea.'

'Don't believe him, Captain Waverley. Fergus holds MacMurrough to be easily Homer's equal, and he would not give up his goatskin purse for a bagful of Louis d'Ors.'

'Well, I must leave you to talk poetry as the elders of Ivor await their hereditary rights of usquebagh.' With which Fergus left the room.

'He means whisky, Captain. The men will insist on stronger liquor as the evening proceeds. Please, sit down. I cannot offer you the water of life but I do have a sweet Rhenish wine.'

Nicolette came forward to pour two glasses from the old Venetian descanter.

'You are very kind, Miss McIvor,' said Waverley raising his glass, 'and your brother was not teasing. I was very struck by the Bard's eloquence.'

'Have you studied much in literature?'

'A great deal. I was not able to attend school in England because of my family's beliefs, so I was educated by a tutor and by living in my uncle's library at Waverley Honour. Yet despite its many volumes I do not remember reading anything of Highland literature.'

'That is because it is more spoken than written. MacMurrough and his kind have extraordinary powers of memory to which they are trained from an early age.'

'What are their poems about?'

'The feats of heroes, woes of lovers, cattle raids, as you already know, and the wars of contending tribes. These are the entertainment at every Highland fireside, and were those poems to be translated into the European languages, I believe they would be a sensation.'

'As you say, I have experienced the cattle raid – the creagh as Evan Dhu calls it – and the pursuit. Our parley with Donald Lean the raider took place in a cave on the lakeside which could only be reached by boat.'

'Did you meet Donald's lovely daughter, Captain Waverley?'

'I was kindly waited on, Miss McIvor, by a very handsome Highland lass.'

'Lassies, indeed, Captain – you are turning native, even on your first visit.'

Waverley smiled and blushed at the same time. There was something retiring and winning in his delicate features. The even nose, high forehead and finely modelled chin were set in motion by eyes as deep brown in colour as his neatly tied hair was light. Having discarded the officer's standard white wig, Waverley looked, natural and at ease with the tan that life in the hills was already conferring on his well bred skin.

'And what about the Bard's song this evening? Am I right in thinking there was some reference to me in the verses?'

'There was – amidst a catalogue of names and praisings. The Bards can extemporise new verses on the wing of the moment in response to the situation.'

'I would like to know what he said about me, if you –'

'And you shall, Captain Waverley, but not here. You must encounter the Highland muse in her proper setting. Nicolette, fetch Calum to carry the clarsach. We have no garden here but nature herself provides the perfect theatre.'

Within minutes a small procession left the Castle by a side gate, bypassing the wild merriment in the hall. Flora went first, wrapped warmly in her plaid. Next came Waverley, carefully steered by Nicolette onto a narrow footpath. Calum, a kilted clansman, brought up the rear shouldering a harp much larger than the one MacMurrough had held in the crook of his arm by the fireside. The accompanying stool was in his free hand.

Dusk was beginning to descend as the party made its way up the steep slope above Castle McIvor on its eastern side, where the edge of the valley came close to the tower. Soon the path began to wind between rocky outcrops causing everyone to carefully mind their footfall. After a while the ascent twisted past a massive boulder and unexpectedly led onto an enclosed glade of stunted trees. For some time the climbers' route had been following a burn which clattered down the hill but the stream now levelled out, stretching across the natural enclosure towards a precipitous rock face down which poured a tumult of pure water.

Flora seemed to know her spot and gestured to Calum to set down stool and clarsach at this edge of the grove, where the roar of the waterfall was softened by distance. Without further ado she took up position at her instrument.

'Now, Captain Waverley, I shall attempt MacMurrough's ode in English, accompanied by the true muses of all Highland bardachd – wind and water.'

The young Englishman stood speechless by the burn as the performance began. Nicolette cowered beneath the trees, a position which was guaranteed to attract every insect the evening had so far hatched to her soft skin.

Mist darkens the mountain,
Night creeps through the vale,

But darker by far is the sleep of the Gael.
The targe and the sword are hidden by dust,
The bloodless claymore reddened with rust.

But the black hours of dark and of sleep are past
Dawn on our mountain is shining at last –
Glenaladale's peaks are lit by the rays,
The streams of Glenfinnan afire with the blaze.

Flora's singing voice was mellow but distinctly articulated.
She glided harmoniously into a catalogue of Highland
clans responsive to the Jacobite cause, followed by the
standard praises of Clan McIvor. In between the two,
she repeated MacMurrough's verse about Waverley, who
blushed more deeply than ever at hearing himself described
as a Gaelic hero. Finally Flora took up the brosnachadh
rhythm, summoning those heroes for conquest or death.

Be the torch of each chieftain like Fionn the fair
The blood in his veins like fierce streaming fire.
Break the base foreign chains as your fathers before,
Spill blood to break free, and bear it no more.

There were further verses on similar lines, but suddenly a
huge deerhound loped into the clearing followed quickly
by Fergus, who seemed as fresh as the dog and unaffected
by the feasting.

'I knew I would find you here. Have you drunk deep
from the Muse's spring, Waverley?'

As he spoke, Fergus bent down and scooped a handful
of the fast flowing stream to his mouth.

'I have been beautifully instructed in the mysteries of the
Highland Bard,' Waverley responded bowing courteously
towards Flora.

'No mystery there, believe me. MacMurrough has now consumed a pint of my best whisky to counteract, he says, the chill of the claret. Anyway Bran and I have come to fetch you back. Dancing is called but the pipers refuse to play unless the lady of the house takes the floor.'

'And all you can offer them, Fergus, is a poor sister.'

'And a poor chief, but the fortunes of our house are once more on the turn. It lies with us to seize the moment.'

Awaiting neither reply nor reaction, Fergus whistled on Bran and led the way back down to Castle McIvor. The great table had been shoved back, and clansmen were already forming up for a reel. It seemed that for Waverley the evening's instruction in Gaelic customs was set to continue.

The next day a message was sent down with Calum to the Baron of Bradwardine, announcing that Waverley would stay at the Castle for a fortnight. Fergus was talking of a traditional gathering for the deer hunt, and the English guest had begun to take a serious interest in Flora's lessons on Highland culture. As if to emphasise he was on official leave from his regiment in Dundee, Waverley abandoned his uniform in favour of tartan trews and a plain jacket. After mornings spent walking and riding, he would join Flora in her drawing room, with or without Fergus, depending on the chief's daily business.

'You would be well entertained at Tullyveolan, Captain Waverley.'

'Arriving there was like a family reunion, so far back does the friendship of our two houses stretch. My Uncle and the Baron served together in the Rising of 1715, as you probably know.'

'He talks of it often.'

'The Baron is very distinctive – a remarkable man. He

overflows with classical learning, and protocols from his soldiering on the continent.'

'He is a true European, the very type of the old cavalier. I often heard his name mentioned in the Palazzo Muti in Rome when I was young.'

'Not more often than Clan McIvor,' interposed Fergus, who was standing looking out of the narrow window.

'You are Europeans as well,' said Waverley.

'I was in service to Her Majesty Clementina Sobieski, and then in the exiled household of King James.'

'But now we have come home,' added Fergus turning his full attention to the conversation. 'What did you think of Rose Bradwardine, Waverley?'

'Miss Rose is an amiable and lovely hostess, perfect in her manners and her nature.'

'And in her form, would you not say?'

'Most of all in her affections,' countered Flora firmly. 'Whoever is fortunate enough to win them will have an invaluable and lasting treasure. Her very soul is homely and rooted in quiet virtue. Her husband will be the focus of all her care and solicitude, as her father is now. She will sympathise with his sorrows, divert his fatigue and share in his pleasures. She will be connected to the world only through him. But he must be a man of virtue, for married to someone cold or negligent she would bend to his mood and die of unkindness. If I were a queen, Captain Waverley, I would command the best youth of the kingdom to woo Rose Bradwardine.'

Waverley seemed nonplussed by Flora's warmth, but not Fergus.

'Well, sister queen, I wish you would command her to accept my hand in marriage.'

'Yours, brother? No, you have another bride, Honour. And the dangers you must run in pursuit of her rival would break poor Rose's heart.'

On another day, Fergus was out visiting some neighbouring chief and the talk turned to political affairs.

'What is your impression of Scotland?' asked Flora.

'It seems a divided country. In Dundee they are all for the Presbyterian Kirk and King George, but not far away at Tullyveolan everyone seems devoted to the exiled Stuarts.'

'Perhaps if their king returned home the nation would unite,' suggested Flora.

'I cannot say, Miss McIvor, honour requires my present loyalty.'

'Of course, Captain Waverley, yet circumstances can change.'

The young man looked down towards the fire, his cheeks reddening in the glow.

'Sometimes, since coming to Scotland, I feel my whole life hanging in the balance.'

How young and vulnerable the heir of Waverley Honour seemed. He too had lost a mother, and by his own account saw little of his father. But there, thought Flora, the comparison ended, for life in a prosperous and sheltered English estate bore little resemblance to the Jacobite Court.

'We must await events,' she counselled.

'What events? In Dundee there the talk was of an imminent rising. Your brother has a regiment of his own here in arms.'

'I am not party to Fergus' thoughts, but his clansmen keep law and order in this region, despite Donald Lean and his banditti.'

'Of course, forgive me, I did not mean to question your –'

'Please, Captain Waverley, don't apologise. I am as

anxious as you to know how things will turn out. I cannot conceal that my dearest wish is that our rightful king be restored.'

'I understand your feelings. I was brought up with them.'

'But here you see why our passions run so deep. There is a way of life, a whole civilisation at stake.'

'Forgive me, I do not fully understand but I would like to learn.'

'Then we must take up poetry again instead of dynastic struggles.'

'Nothing would please me more.'

This was a cue for the clarsach to be brought out and tea served.

As these leisurely days passed in the glen, any sense of imminent crisis waned. Clan McIvor seemed to have dispersed further afield, and the afternoon lessons lengthened as the weather became warmer.

Nearly three weeks had gone by when Fergus announced that the hunt had been arranged. The gathering of clans for a communal deer drive was an ancient Highland tradition, as Flora explained. But it appeared that this year's assembly was to be the largest in a generation. No chief worthy of his lineage would be absent. Flora McIvor insisted on going with her brother and Waverley to the rendezvous. They were accompanied by a small army of McIvor clansman in full regalia.

Neither Flora nor Waverley understood the geography of their journey north, but it took them into an ever widening landscape of mountains and high glens. The meeting place was at the confluence of two valleys beneath a spectacular precipice, where the foaming rivers met. Yet in the mouth of both glens were green slopes ideal for camping, rich in pasture and abundant fresh water. Flora described these as sheilings, though the temporary shelters erected by the clans were on a scale far removed from the humble pastoral shelters she had seen the previous summer. Pine trees were cut and trimmed to create long rafters dressed with fir branches and heather. Rough hewn benches and tables were set up beneath these canopies to accommodate the numbers of clansmen, along with the copious quantities of meat and drink required for their nightly entertainment.

Waverley kept close to Flora, since he could not follow the run of conversation nor keep up with the McIvor's whirlwind diplomacy. The chiefs in general seemed to be in constant motion receiving and bestowing hospitality. Support was being canvassed for armed revolt against the Hanoverian regime in London, but Flora was careful to conceal this from Waverley. As one of the few women present it was easy for her to avoid private discussions and bring the young Englishman to social gatherings. Moreover her ties with the Jacobite Court made her reluctant to enter into speculation about the intentions of King James and his more unpredictable son and heir, Charles Edward Stuart.

The plan was that those chiefs who committed to the rising would meet further north when the hunt was concluded. Flora would return to Castle McIvor with Waverley and accompany him back to Tullyveolan to visit Rose.

After three days of feasting, the chiefs were at last called out with their retinues to take up position for the main business of the hunt. Flora and Waverley were amongst those drawn up at the mouth of the glens which rose steadily northward. The gillies had been out in force since before dawn with their dogs, spreading across the neighbouring hills and glens in order to gather in the maximum possible number of deer. Forming a wide-flung ring they gradually tightened their trap, driving the disturbed animals before them.

The huntsmen were positioned at the foot of the valley and on its near sides, along which hurdles had been erected so that the herds would be channelled towards the marksmen. As Flora waited amongst the chiefs she could hear a rising clamour of dogs, men shouting and some musket shots. The first deer appeared amidst foxes, hares and a few startled goats, breaking over the slope in twos and threes. They were picked off at long range by those with the keenest aim.

Then in a few moments the upper ridge of the glen was a thicket of antlers. The foremost animals appeared to pause as following hinds massed behind them. Flora had never seen so many deer. She exchanged a glance with Waverley who was astonished at the sight and flushed with excitement. Fergus was several paces to the fore with the musket butt already at his shoulder.

As if by silent decision, the ridge moved becoming a wave of cantering flesh. Firing burst out on all sides, dogs were unleashed and commands were lost in the mêlée. But something was wrong, and the more experienced huntsmen sensed it. Instead of scattering before fire, the deer kept coming. The canter burst into a gallop and the massed herd charged towards their enemy sweeping the flimsy hurdles aside. With cries of alarm weapons were thrown aside, heedless of rank or dignity, and chiefs flung themselves onto the ground letting the deer pound over them.

But Waverley did not understand the warning shouts and stood his ground, only to be hurled down bodily by Fergus who pressed him flat with an iron grip as the deer trampled onwards. The horde hurtled past and thundered into the lower glen. Flora picked herself up and hurried towards the prostrate Englishman. Soon others were at her side turning Waverley gently over. He was writhing with pain. Then under Fergus's supervision four men lifted him on their linked arms and bore him rapidly off to a shelter.

The physician was called and Waverley was cupped, bled and dosed with a herbal infusion. Each stage of the treatment was accompanied with muttered incantations, and every so often a full voiced melodious chant. Waverley fell into a restive sleep, though not before multiple contusions, cuts and a broken ankle had been catalogued. Flora sat by the heather couch until it was clear that the patient was not fevered before going to find her brother.

Fergus was pacing up and down under the McIvor canopy, wearing the expression with which Flora had been familiar since childhood. He did not like his plans disarranged.

'The Englishman will not be able to travel back tomorrow.'

'He was lucky to escape with his life, Fergus – only your quick thinking prevented him being gored.'

'I have to go north, but Waverley could rest at our cousin McKeachen's house till he can ride. Someone will need to look after him.'

There was a silence as Fergus came to a halt, looking directly at Flora.

'Has McKeachen no retainers?'

'I am sure Waverley would prefer a gentler attendant, and in this case so would I, Flora.'

'What interest do you have in the matter?'

'Don't be awkward. You know that we must persuade Waverley to join the rising. This could be a perfect opportunity.'

'I know no such thing, Fergus. I do not keep my loyalties secret – influence whom they may – but I shall not apply pressure to make anyone act dishonourably against their own principles.'

'I am not speaking of pressure.'

'Then of what are you speaking?'

'Don't be naive, Flora, you can see that he is smitten.'

'I see no such thing. How can you even suggest it, and with the same breath urge me to be nurse at his bedside? I shall return to Castle McIvor tomorrow as arranged. Calum can stay with Waverley at McKeachen's until your business in the north is concluded. God willing, your persuasions there will be successful. Everything depends on the northern clans coming out.'

Before Fergus could disagree or comment, Flora left the shelter, staying out in the cooling air until the feasting commenced. However the day's events, not least the injuries suffered by an honoured guest, seemed to have lowered the general good spirits. Thoughts were turning towards the difficult decisions ahead.

The next morning Flora returned to Castle McIvor. She took no farewell of Waverley whom she understood to be weak but comfortable. On arrival she immediately sent word to Rose Bradwardine that any visit to Tullyveolan would have to be delayed.

The old tower seemed very quiet due to the absence of the clansmen in the north, but the chief's sister established a quiet routine with the remaining servants, and waited for news. As far as Flora could remember, she had longed for the return of the Stuarts to Scotland, and for her own homecoming. Now both events appeared to be happening at the same time. These inactive days were a chance to come to terms with the speed of events.

Could the impetuous Charles Edward be relied on to lead this expedition, and would the French actually allow him to leave for Scotland? Flora could imagine the letters weighted with caution that would be coming north from the Palazzo Muti. King James was not beyond encouraging the French to restrain his disaffected son, if he knew where Charles was and what he was intending. The prince was not beyond acting on his own initiative regardless of James' vacillations. If a campaign started Fergus would soon be embroiled in the politics of its leadership. Pray God the rising would begin soon, for the Highland clans could not afford to be in readiness for long, or to risk further sanctions.

As for Waverley, Flora went back over their conversations to see if she had given any misleading signal. She thought not, yet she had tried to encourage his patriotic feelings. Was it Fergus who had thrown him some kind of hint or encouragement, and slewed his reactions? She would now have to be doubly on guard, for she had no intention of marriage, whatever Fergus might hope for Clan McIvor's fortunes. Flora was determined to follow events at firsthand, and if possible play her own part.

As the week dragged on the messenger came back from Tullyveolan with letters for Waverley and newspapers for Fergus. Then on the sixth day they appeared together without warning, coming slowly down the glen. The Englishman was riding on a pony and though pale was able to dismount and limp into the hall leaning on a stick. One look at Fergus was enough to show that there was important news, but both men dispersed to read their mail without comment. There was no sign of the armed clansmen. Flora went back to her rooms and summoned Nicolette to help lay out a worktable so that the women could begin making white cockades.

But within a short time, Waverley and then hard on his heels Fergus burst into the drawing room, scattering the work party.

'Look at this,' cried Waverley, 'throwing a letter onto the table. 'Three days' notice revoking my leave. Sent more than two weeks ago. What sort of treatment is that from a fellow officer?'

'My dear Waverley,' added Fergus, 'someone is determined on your disgrace. Look.'

He passed over the London paper which reported Waverley's demotion from his captaincy following absence without leave.

'What can I do? My commanding officer has not even waited on reply. It is so dishonourable and unfair.' He seemed on the verge of tears.

'It is their fear of rebellion, Waverley. You must write resigning your commission, but clearly marking the date you first received this letter.'

'You are right, Fergus.'

'But if I were you, I would revenge myself on unjust authority by renouncing allegiance to the House of Hanover. This is a clear signal for action.' Fergus picked up a cockade and offered it to Waverley. 'Change your colours.'

The now former officer took off his bonnet and removed the regimental plume that he wore pinned at the front. 'The king who gave me this badge has himself removed it, in a way that leaves me little reason to regret his service. Miss McIvor, will you attach a new cockade to my hat?'

'No, Mr Waverley, I cannot sew such favours on the impulse of a moment. Not until you have time to reflect more carefully on this choice.'

'Miss McIvor does not think this soldier worthy of this

favour or of her cause?'

'Not at all,' responded Flora soothingly, 'why would I refuse my brother's friend when I am enlisting every man of honour in the cause? But you, Mr Waverley, are far from home and in danger of making a life or death decision in a mood of resentment. You must pause before plunging into this enterprise.'

Fergus had to turn away to bite back his furious retort. Waverley stood nonplussed and uncertain.

'Well, sister, I must leave you to your new role as mediator between the Elector of Hanover and the subjects of your loyal sovereign and benefactor.'

Then he stalked out, and Waverley sank gratefully into a chair.

'Please forgive me. I did not mean to cause any...'

'My brother is unjust. He can bear no obstacle that interrupts or thwarts his zeal.'

'Do you not share his faith?'

'If anything mine is greater, if that is possible.' Flora looked away, as if considering some further confession, then recalled herself. 'Though I am not caught up like him in the urgency of military preparations. He is driven and impatient. But a true and just cause, Mr Waverley, can only be advanced by true and just means. So you must make your own decision calmly with proper time to reflect.'

'Miss McIvor, what would I do without you? You are my true monitor and guardian... Could I hope, could I dare to think that you could be an affectionate friend, a companion to redeem my errors and guide my future life?'

During this speech Waverley had taken hold of Flora's hand, which was firmly withdrawn.

'I fear I am a creature of unstable imagination, and not of reason, swayed by the latest emotion.' His hand was reaching out again.

'Sir, you are allowing your joy at escaping the recruiting officer to overcome you.'

'Flora, you cannot mistake the meaning of my feelings. Allow me to speak to your brother –'

'Not for the world, Mr Waverley.'

'Is there some fatal bar – are your emotions pledged elsewhere?'

'I have not considered anyone with reference to this subject.'

'Give me time for us to become better known to each other.'

'Your nature is open for all to see, Mr Waverley. You must be satisfied with my resolution.'

To this, the aspiring suitor had no answer, and silence reigned.

Flora had stood up to go when Fergus barged into the interview in its dying moments.

'Come down to the courtyard, and you'll see a sight worth all he tirades of your Romances. A hundred firelocks and as many broadswords, sent by our friends, and as many stout fellows almost fighting to possess them. What ails you, Waverley? Anyone would say you'd had the evil eye put on you. Never mind my sister, Edward, for the wisest of her sex are fools in the main business of life.'

'On the contrary, your sister is only too reasonable.'

'Enough, I vouch Flora will be as unreasonable as any by tomorrow. Now come and see these weapons.'

The disconsolate Waverley hobbled out in Fergus' wake, leaving Flora tight lipped and in possession of the field.

The next few days continued under uneasy truce. More messengers arrived at Castle McIvor and further consignments of weapons. There was open speculation that Prince Charles Edward had already landed in the Western Isles of Scotland, and that a French invasion was expected hourly on the southern coast of England.

Then a messenger arrived from Tullyveolan, carrying a letter from Rose Bradwardine. It was a warning. Her father the Baron had left with some retainers to join the Jacobite muster, and the house had been occupied by Government troops with a warrant to arrest Waverley. He was touched by Rose's concern for his safety even in the midst of her own troubles. This prompted the decision he had been avoiding since his rejection by Flora.

'I must leave for Edinburgh to seek out some of my family's connections, and clear myself of any military wrongdoing. Then I will return to assist Rose at Tullyveolan in her father's absence.'

'A wise and kind resolution,' acknowledged Flora immediately.

'You're running your head into the lion's mouth,' countered her brother, 'for you don't understand the severity of a government under threat. I will have to rescue you from some dungeon in Stirling or Edinburgh Castle.'

'My innocence and my rank will be sufficient protection.'

'The friends you count on may be taken up with their own affairs in such a crisis. Take the plaid, I beg you, and stay here amidst the mist and crows, for the bravest cause in which sword was ever drawn.'

'I must be excused, dear Fergus, and run my own risk.'

'You are determined. Well, you will have the brown mare to ride safely on, and the protection of McIvor as far as my word is law.'

'I thank you for your generosity. I'll go and pack my things.'

Waverley was moving more nimbly now though still

with the aid of a stick.

'He's a fool.'

'Is he really in such danger?' asked Flora anxiously.

'Don't worry, I'll put Donald Lean's bloodhounds on his scent. I have a feeling that we have not seen the last of your young gallant.'

2

FLORA STOOD AT the window looking down the avenue of trees. It was cold in the room though the fire had already been lit. A pale winter sun was rising over the fields beyond the gates, and lighting up the bare garden ground.

It was two months since Flora had last stayed at Bannockburn House, on the army's journey south. But it felt more like two years. So much had happened. She and Rose had been guests then of the laird Hugh Paterson, not of his niece, Clementina. Strange to find another Clementina here in Scotland, named for Flora's long dead benefactress. Clementina's father, John Walkinshaw, had rescued the Sobieski princess in Poland and brought her across Europe to marry James the rightful Stuart king of Scotland, England and Ireland.

This time though there was something more familiar to Flora in her surroundings. She was becoming accustomed to the domestic solidity of Scotland's buildings and landscape. The house was a Scots laird's substitute for the castles of old. Spacious yet intimate, the sturdy native stones were set to good effect within the folds of valleys, woods and open fields quite unlike the sweeping heights in which Castle McIvor sat like a nesting eagle. Moreover the compact living quarters were surrounded by gardens. Despite the wintry conditions Flora could see the shapes of fruit trees, shrubberies, and herb beds.

Flora was continually amazed by the open changing light. Whatever the weather, in Lowlands or Highlands, you could watch the atmosphere shifting over distant hills and before your eyes. The skies were always big and flowing. In Italy, despite the blazing suns of summer, Flora had lived enclosed at Palazzo Muti, in the Convent, and then again back in service in the shuttered rooms of that narrow overshadowed mansion in the cramped street of Rome. As she looked, sunlight was dispersing flimsy mists from the lower ground and starting a new day.

Flora sighed as she turned back towards the fire pulling the shawl tighter round her shoulders. Rose would appear soon and then later Clementina. Breakfast would be served next door, thick oatmeal porridge with dried fruits, tea, fresh bannocks, butter and honey. What would the prince's army be eating today in England, camped perhaps on open ground, exposed to frost and snow? Would there be any news from the south? Had they evaded Wade's troops, after the capture of Carlisle? Had they passed Manchester on the road to London, or would Cumberland's forces block their progress?

Waiting for news of other places and of someone else's actions seemed to be the confining fate of women. And Flora resented the restriction. Fortunately Rose arrived to dispel her mood. Tall and willowy with fair colouring, shining cheeks and ready blushes Rose dispensed goodwill with easy naturalness. She stooped to kiss Flora and give her a morning hug.

'Ugh it is cold. How do you always manage to be up first? Let's go to breakfast now. It could be ages before Clementina comes.'

The morning parlour was a cosy corner room, and soon Flora and Rose were comfortably settled round a small table laden with bowls, cups and jugs. Within a few minutes Rose made her first mention that day of Edward Waverley.

'I hope Waverley is wearing the warm trews and his double breasted jacket. It was very generous of him to serve as a volunteer in Fergus' regiment, but it means he will be travelling on foot and he cannot have been used to walking all the time as a boy. Is it not more dangerous on foot as well?'

'Your father's cavalry troop is often in danger, scouting ahead or hurrying to a danger spot where there has been some surprise attack.'

'That is true, God preserve him, but my dear father is bred to it. He has been a soldier all his days. He lives and breathes campaigns.'

Including long past and forgotten ones thought Flora. The Baron was a tall upright figure whose conversation was a perpetual catalogue of military history, classical allusions and chivalric etiquette. Had it not been for his proven skill and experience in the field, the old cavalier might have become the object of humour, though few would have risked offending the Baron to his face, for he loved nothing better than rapiers drawn on some point of honour.

'Waverley was a serving officer too before declaring for the prince.'

'Yes, he has come home to his true loyalty, Flora. His aunt and uncle are very proud of their nephew, though his father as you know has been a political trimmer.'

'I understand that Waverley is the heir to his uncle's title and estate.'

'If our king is restored then good fortune should be his.'

Flora smiled inwardly at Rose's unguarded affection.

She had no idea of Waverley's declaration of love at Castle McIvor. Nor, apart from some initial embarrassment, had Waverley shown any hint of his earlier suit, when he had arrived at the prince's newly captured headquarters in Edinburgh. Having set out for Scotland's capital as a suspect keen to clear his Hanoverian name, Waverley had been arrested by a magistrate and dispatched for trial. Next he had been freed in an ambush, almost certainly contrived by Donald Lean, and then captured once more, this time by a troop of volunteers on their way to join the Jacobite army.

Needless to say, on arrival in Edinburgh, Waverley had been embraced by Fergus like a long lost brother, and presented immediately to the prince. Aware of the importance of English supporters, Charles had warmly welcomed the young heir to Waverly Honour without presuming on his personal loyalty. This instantly had the desired effect. Waverley swore his allegiance on the spot and, tactfully refusing the offer of a commission, volunteered to serve with Fergus. A grateful Charles provided Waverley with weapons suitable to his status, and before the day was out Fergus had the tall Englishman fully dressed and equipped as a Highland gentleman at arms.

Clementina came in rubbing her eyes but full of morning brio. She called the company, reduced as it was, to order.

'So, what will His Majesty do today, ladies? Inspect the troops camping in the Royal Park, then consult his Council, have dinner, and next – serious business of the day – command a ball at Holyrood, followed by supper. Every loyal lady of Edinburgh will be there, not to mention all the wives and sweethearts of his followers who have hurried to the capital filling every lodging in Auld Reekie.

What shall we wear to rout them all?'

She was irresistible in this mood, conjuring the heady weeks of August and September back into life. It was for those days of royal restoration, in the social whirl of the capital, that Clementina had been born. The spark lit up her sharp face with its upturned nose and luminous brown eyes beneath the curls. Her skin was slightly freckled and vivacious. Was she dark or fair? It did not matter, since Clementina slipped between conventions taking everyone with her in a breathless rush. There was though no mistaking her height and will to lead.

'Enough, enough, sit down and eat something and your brain will settle,' chided Flora.

The new arrival hugged both of her friends and set to work on a hearty breakfast.

'It's a fine day despite the season,' she munched, 'shall we take a walk?'

'I would rather keep indoors,' ventured Rose.

'Why? The servants will be here if any message arrives.'

'Still, I would like to wait, and write some letters. To my father.'

'Of course, Rose,' said Flora, 'you must have peace to write. Clementina will drag me off into the country, whatever the risk. We may be seized by some sally from the castle garrison, but I am game to explore, and she cannot be contained.'

So the day's schedule was agreed, though the three young women were all in their own ways marking time, waiting on news that might make or break their whole lives. Despite her father's resolute commitment to the cause, Rose's feelings were more personal than political. Flora's convictions overrode or at least directed her emotions. Clementina was a natural gambler, whose whole life had been caught up in the Stuart enterprise.

She might appear mercurial and unpredictable, but there was unwavering ardour beneath her surface moods. She played to win.

The wind had freshened by the time Flora and Clementina headed out on foot, refusing any escort. They went down the tree lined avenue and out of the gates into an area of woodland. Climbing through the trees they emerged on a ridge into a blast of cold air, which also had the effect of clearing the view. On their right lay the village of Bannockburn straggling towards the defile through which that small river ran. Due north, Stirling Castle peaked out above succeeding ridges. To the north east the Ochil Hills rose bluntly from the Carse of Stirling, already topped with a dusting of white snow.

'That is the Borestone, where Robert the Bruce's army mustered.' Clementina pointed northwest towards a low hill. 'It's near the Milton of St Ninians, not Bannockburn. But people here say the battle was fought there, beyond the village on level ground between the Bannock and the Pelham Burns.'

'Where is the Sheriffmuir?'

'There,' Clementina's long arm shot out again, 'you can see the Ochils level down into the muirland.'

'My father fought at Sherriffmuir. I never thought I would see the place for myself.'

'This is the place for battles, Flora. You can't traverse Scotland without coming by Stirling.'

'And the Castle is still in enemy hands.'

'For now. Besieging castles is a long business.'

'And the prince needs quick victories, to follow Prestonpans.'

'I can't believe I missed it,' complained Clementina. 'Tell me what it was like.'

'I told you, several times.'

'Tell me again.'

'It wasn't pleasant, Clementina. Even though we could see the tactics spread out beneath us. When the Jacobite troops found their way through the marsh and formed up, Cope's army had to turn and regroup. You could see they were unsettled, even at that distance. And then the Highlanders charged like a rushing wave – we could hear the yells as loud as the gunfire. The red ranks broke and fled within minutes.'

'No English army can face a Highland charge. That is our secret weapon!'

'The English troops were piling into the defiles desperately trying to get away, like sheep driven by wolves. The prince and his officers rode out to restrain the clansmen, ensuring quarter for the wounded and the prisoners. It could have been a shambles, Clementina, for I must confess that our Highlanders have a bloodlust when the heat of battle rises in them.'

'But it was the decisive victory, Flora, unexpected and total. It turned the tables, when everyone said the prince was a hopeless adventurer.'

'Maybe. Yet look at these villages and farms. This is a different Scotland, Clementina, from the clan territories. Do they support a Stuart restoration?'

'When we win, they might. But it's true, the majority are not Jacobite in the Lowlands, apart from some loyal families. It is because of religion. They see Charles as a Papist threatening their Presbyterian kirks and schools. Aye and their Presbyterian pockets. That really is a matter of godliness.' Clementina's irony dissolved into giggles. 'The Minster at St Ninian's came to see Uncle Hugh before he left, to deliver a rebuke on the ungodly disturbance of trade by heathen Jacobites.'

'What did your Uncle say?'

'He said, "Aye, Minister, it may be a judgement on our backsliding." That dried the Reverend up as he couldn't guess what was meant. Sanctimonious prig. No nation could thrive with a religion like that.'

'So must the prince restore Catholicism?'

'Speak it not in Gath! We have the perfect compromise in the Episcopal faith, Flora. Protestant yet Christian, and acceptable to England. The prince is no fool.'

'You have studied his character closely?'

'Only by acquaintance, in Edinburgh.'

'But he charmed everyone there, Clementina. Are you swayed by charm, even in religion?'

'Yes, Flora, yes. You know I love the court life – dancing and music and costumes, and the intrigues and campaign. Why should I be left out when it is my family's birthright?'

'There are certainly more than enough intrigues, and squabbles. I just hope they do not ruin the expedition through divided councils.'

There was no answer to that, and the two turned along the ridge, gaining a clearer view of the solid Ochils as they walked. Eventually they turned back towards the house, coming past a square dovecot into the garden and finally inside to warming broth by the fireside.

Flora sat on her own in the parlour after lunch. Rose was resting in her room while Clementina was downstairs gossiping and interfering with the running of the house. The Exercises of St Ignatius lay unopened on the arm of her chair. It was strange how in this land without priests the devotional habits of a lifetime fell away so easily. Before the Church had given her restricted existence a pattern, depth perhaps, but now events were happening daily without any predictable shape.

The weeks in Edinburgh had been unlike anything Flora had experienced, though she suspected that was true of everyone at the prince's improvised Court. Charles was at the centre of it all, wholly changed from the spirited rebellious child of the Palazzo Muti. Apart from his pudgy cheeks and chin, all his puppy fat had gone. This accentuated his height, and he carried it with energy and command. Yet, like his younger self, Charles still had his feelings close to the surface which gave his manner an attractive openness and charm. And he encouraged everything around him to be full of life and energy with receptions, music, dancing and a constant bustle of meeting and greeting. It was as if everything was to be the opposite of his father's stiff formality, and the austere piety that made the Palazzo such an ordeal for the young.

Yet Flora could see there was another side to this newly adult Charles. Beneath the charm there was reserve and calculation. He knew that winning hearts and minds at Holyrood was essential to his cause, and that Court life must appear to honour everybody, without favouring one faction against another.

For the uprising was mainly held together by Charles' determination, his gambler's instinct. The prince's Irish and French advisers urged caution and based everything on the invasion of England assisted by a French army. The chiefs and most of the Scots Jacobites were intent on restoring the Stuarts in Scotland, so repairing their own traditions and fortunes. Every Highlander was avidly ambitious for personal title and favour. Charles' Secretary, Murray of Broughton, juggled the factions at Council. Charles' military commander Lord George Murray was given only limited authority, and was frequently contradicted by Colonel O'Sullivan, the senior Irish officer. The chiefs jostled for position at Court and on the battlefield. Did

Charles at heart trust anyone?

At least the adventures of Edward Waverley had offered some light relief amidst the tensions. He had blossomed in the atmosphere at Holyrood which allowed his genial, social side full play. He seemed most at home in the company of women, while Rose's growing attachment was obvious for all to see, except Fergus.

After the wholesale victory over Cope, the army delayed in Edinburgh with the mistaken hope of capturing its Castle. Inactivity and court life did not suit Fergus, who had filled this desultory interval with his ambitious plans for Clan McIvor. This involved marriage to Rose Bradwardine, as long as her father could be persuaded to settle his estate on her instead of a distant male relative who had committed the fatal error of remaining on the Hanoverian side. Fergus' trump card in this campaign was the title of Earl that he had been awarded by King James for his loyal services in Europe. He now requested Charles to actively confer that title on his father's behalf. The Baron could not resist alliance with Earldom. As Flora knew, Rose had not been consulted on any count.

Charles however had asked Fergus not to press his just claim to the title at that moment as it would arouse the jealousy of the other chiefs, all of whom would expect some comparable honour. So Fergus had divulged his whole scheme to the prince in order to show why the Earldom was now essential. Flora could recall every word of Fergus' account.

'I was determined to leave him no pretence for ingratitude, so I explained why he could command any other sacrifice at this moment rather than renunciation of my title. I told him my full plan.'

'What plan?' Waverley had asked, his attention gripped.

'Marriage, my dear Waverley, to Rose. And joining my

title to the estate of Tullyveolan.'

'Marriage to Rose?' Waverley was clearly shocked but Fergus was in full flood and brushed him aside.

'What was the prince's answer?' Flora intervened.

'Answer? Curse not the king, Flora. He answered that he was truly glad I had confided in him as that would prevent disappointment. For, on the word of a prince, he knew that Miss Bradwardine's affections were already engaged elsewhere and, moreover, he was under a particular promise to favour them. "So, my dear Fergus," says he, very affable, "as the marriage is out of the question, there is no hurry about the Earldom." And off he floated to flatter someone else's hopes, without reward.'

'What did he mean?' Waverley managed to ask.

'He intends to marry her off to one of his French or Irish entourage, O'Sullivan no doubt. But that man whoever he is had better look out for himself, as I will personally reward him in full measure. I could sell myself to the Devil or the Elector of Hanover if either of them promised revenge.'

Away Fergus stomped in a fury, followed minutes later by a subdued and thoughtful Waverley.

In the end, Flora was sure, Rose and Waverley would find their way to each other. As for Fergus, it was difficult to imagine any third person interrupting their long familiarity and dependence. Fergus was her only family, apart from adoption into the extended household of Palazzo Muti. If and when her brother married, Flora would continue in the same dependent way, as long as the Stuart cause required their service.

Flora sat on by the fire as darkness gathered outside. When a maid came in to close the shutters and light candles, she found Flora dozing lightly her book of prayers still unopened.

The first signs were small parties of stragglers, often no

more than one or two in number, going past the house
on their way north. This was no surprise as the clansmen,
though keen to fight, were equally liable to make off home
if there was plunder to be safeguarded, some slight to their
honour, or crops to harvest. The real surprise was how
disciplined the Highland army had been, marching south.
There were of course no crops to harvest in December, and
as if to prove the point, a hard frost set in with frequent
flurries of snow.

On the 14th of December the snow strengthened and
in the afternoon darkness began to close in around the
drifting white. Three men, ragged and shivering, sought
shelter and were taken into the kitchen. They were Grants
who had come out without their chief, and were now
trying to get home before the mountain passes were shut
down. They were definite that the prince's army had
already turned back for Scotland.

Clementina brought the story upstairs but dismissed
it as the self-justification of deserters. Nonetheless, as
bad weather continued to keep the three young women
indoors, their unease grew. The Grants had left after one
night ready to gamble on their knowledge of the country.
They could smell home even through the storm.

There was however no doubting the next messengers
who arrived two days later. They were a party of Camerons
travelling north at speed and in good order. They were
acting on instruction of their chief, Lochiel, who had been
the first to raise his clan in Charles' cause. Their mission
was to organise supplies and reinforcements in Appin.
The prince was on his way north. Having declared James
King of England at Ashbourne, the army had pushed on a
few miles south of Derby but then turned back. There had
been no battle and no sighting of any of the three armies
that the Hanoverians had in the field. The Camerons

delayed no longer but pushed on taking advantage of temporarily clearing skies. They left anxious speculation in their wake.

'This cannot be the prince's choice – to turn back with London in his sights!' Flora could not imagine Charles giving way of his own free will, not when he was on the verge of realising his consuming ambition, against all the odds. Something else had intervened to thwart him.

'What if English Jacobites are not joining the standard? They would all be in terrible danger.' Rose sat by the fire twisting one hand in the other, with no attempt at composure.

'Don't be feeble, Rose,' rebuked Clementina, 'there is a whole Highland army on the march, with French, Irish and English volunteers. There is more to this than cowardly English Jacobites.'

'In what way?' quizzed Flora.

'Lord George Murray's way. He always thinks he knows better when it comes to tactics, and his heart was never in this expedition into England.'

'Invasion, you mean,' Rose corrected with a sob.

'How can a rightful king invade his own country?' challenged Flora.

'But that's exactly how many English people see it, invasion by a horde of barbarous savages. I'm sorry, Flora, you know that is not how I feel.'

'It's a Scottish army, Rose, Highland and Lowland, as you know,' scolded Clementina.

'But the prince has adopted Highland dress. Edward Waverley explained the English attitude to me, and Scots Lowlanders often feel the same. How will they manage in a hostile country without friends and –'

'Well Prince Charles explained to me,' Clementina cut in again, 'how some people on his Council were determined to prevent any takeover of England.'

'Which people? And why?' demanded Flora. Clementina could be sweeping and vague in the same breath.

'The chiefs. They want Scotland restored to its old self, not another distant king in London.'

'That's not true, not of Fergus anyway. He is determined to win Britain back for the Stuarts, all of it. We've spent our whole lives in that cause.'

Yet even as she countered Clementina's argument, Flora was wondering when the younger woman had become so close to Charles. Close enough it appeared to glean guarded opinions that would cause grave offence if spread abroad. Her mind was running back over the two days they had spent at Bannockburn on the way south, and the extended weeks at Edinburgh. She had not noticed any special intimacy between the prince and Clementina, but then she had not been looking. The Palace of Holyroodhouse had many more chambers than the Palazzo Muti.

'Maybe the Irish or the French advisers are behind it?' Flora wondered aloud.

'Why?' It was Clementina's turn to challenge.

'Because there has been no French invasion? And they counted on it before approaching London.'

'Please,' begged Rose, 'let's stop this. It's pointless. We don't know. All we can do is wait for more news.'

The room subsided into uneasy silence. Flora and Rose took up book and sewing with little sign of attention. Clementina left to go downstairs, hungry for whatever news the next messenger might bring.

The next morning brought no further news but better weather. There was a lightening of the gloomy skies and the wind dropped. When it seemed unlikely that any more messengers would arrive, Flora proposed a walk outside. Rose however again wanted to keep indoors, while Clementina was expending her pent-up energy in rearranging the pantry and annoying housekeeper, cook and maid by turn.

Flora was glad to escape into the solitude of the fields for there was little sign of human life apart from the drifting smoke of cottage fires. Wrapped up tightly against the cold she walked with a firm tread out of the garden towards the hills. The tops were mantled in white as far as the eye could see. To the north, where the Ochils merged into the Highland ranges, the mountains were completely snow bound. Keeping to the higher slopes, Flora swung south till she came back to the main road. Everything was quiet with no sign of movement in either direction. The villages of Carnock and Plean huddled silently against the cold.

The sun was very low now and dusk was gathering. But Flora was not ready to be cooped up again indoors with all the anxieties and frictions, so she followed the road past the back of the house and started out towards Stirling. At the top of the next ridge, castle and town were revealed on their rocky citadel, catching the last gleams from the west. Flora stood for a while tracing the contours of the ramparts, and was about to turn back for the house when a movement caught her eye.

In the dip below her a small stream ran towards the Bannockburn. Across it ran a wooden bridge, offering a short cut into the Milton. Someone was below the bridge. As Flora moved carefully down the slope on the steep path towards the mill, she could see that it was a woman in dark clothes bent over the water. She appeared to be washing something in the icy stream. The path turned into a scatter of trees, and when Flora emerged again into view there was no sign of the woman. Flora went all the way to the bridge wondering where the dark figure had gone, and looked down in to the fiercely flowing burn.

It was odd to be doing laundry outdoors on such a day. How had the woman disappeared so quickly? At least she had not fallen into those icy waters. And as Flora peered the atmosphere around her seemed to mirror the black currents. She felt suddenly chilled. Shaking herself into action, she climbed back up the path casting a few glances behind her, and within a short time she was knocking her boots clear of snow at the kitchen door.

Flora was drying herself at the kitchen fire when Clementina appeared.

'Do the poor people wash clothes in the mill stream?' she asked, rubbing at her plaid.

'Maybe in the summer but not in this weather. Why?'

'I saw a woman at the bridge. I thought she was washing something.'

Clementina looked at her strangely. 'The main ford used to be there across the Bannockburn. There are stories about –'

They were distracted by a scratching sound at the door. It became more urgent – mixed sobs and whimpers of distress. Clementina pulled the door open and a man crawled into the room, panting and sodden, but Flora knew him immediately for Calum.

'Miss Flora, Miss Flora.' He reached out blindly.

'Calum, I'm here. It's me, Flora. Tell me.'

'McIvor's taken, taken by the redcoats.'

'And the others, what of the others?'

'Ewan Dhu fallen. By his side. We would not leave him.'

'The Baron, Calum, and Waverley?'

'The Baron was not there. The Englishman is lost. Into the country, after the fight. I came at once... as fast as I was able.'

The house keeper joined Flora beside the exhausted man with a flask of whisky in her hand, forcing some drops between his lips.

'What fight, Calum?'

'Not the prince, Miss Flora. We would never be leaving him. Fight without... McIvor fallen.'

The head fell back on Flora's arm. For now he could say no more.

It emerged that Calum had run most of the way north, barely stopping for brief snatches of sleep. Carrying oatmeal in a leather pouch, and using cold water from streams, he had avoided any human contact until, half-dead with exhaustion, he reached his destination, Flora. It was tribute to his tenacity and endurance that by the succeeding afternoon, Calum was upright in the back parlour ready to tell the full story. His listeners had already received the main disastrous news, but they were nevertheless anxious to absorb every detail.

As the slight, wiry figure drew himself to his full height, Flora was reminded of Calum's role at Castle McIvor as fireside storyteller, reciting clan tales, historical legends, or stories of the fairy people for the entertainment of the chief's family and household. He had often stood by the hearth in Flora's drawing room in the same way. Yet his recitation now was no fable but an immediate matter of life or death. Pushing back a tangle of matted hair, Calum began with an apology.

'You will be forgiving, gentle ladies, my poor dress, and the bearing of such news, to the grief of our clan and the name of McIvor. But it was destined for such things to be, and it is being God's hands.'

Nobody spoke in case it delayed the narration. The reaction of the three young women was to lean forward more attentively.

'The army of Prince Charles was at Manchester where the prince wished to be stopping for some days, to prevent the rumour that he was retreating. But McIvor was angry, in a rage of despair, blaming the Council of War, the Lord George and the prince himself for turning back from London. "The prize was in our grasp," he was always saying to Euan Dhu, "for the Sassenach would be fleeing before us."

'But there was no help from the people of that city, and the redcoats were pressing upon us. So Lord George gave the marching orders, and the prince remained in his quarters until all was drawn up, and then rode to the front, rarely walking with his people as he was used to doing when we went to Derby.

'But, truth to be telling, it was Lord George had the right hold of it, for we saw their horsemen in the distance, scouting against our rear. Now, your ladyships, I must be telling you that Clan McIvor are at the rear of the army, where all the bravest are found, along with Glengarry of MacDonell and Cluny the MacPherson with their kinsmen. So we saw the mounted redcoats buzzing like hornets on our flanks.

'The prince is then at Lancaster and the men of the clans were all ready to fight as we did at the saltpans on Forth. Cumberland is the one we must be fighting and the prince agreed to the loyal protest of McIvor and all the chiefs. So Lord George and the Chevalier O'Sullivan chose ground for the battle with his Lordship saying that never was a better field for Highlanders seen since the Pans. But again the prince would be changing his mind and ordering a march to Kendal. Only a great many of the carriages and the four-wheeled carts could not be got forward because of the steepness of the hill and the badness of the road and the rain coming on with some turning to sleet and the churning of the track. For the wagons were too big for the roads, and too heavy on account of being weighed down with ammunition.

'And Lord George went to the prince and to O'Sullivan to ask for more men and they were drinking in their quarters and not able to assist till the morning came. Now it rained all the night and we slept out in our plaids, and at first light the Manchester volunteers came to help and we were there, McIvor and Glengarry with Cluny MacPherson. And we were up to our middle in water, pushing and pulling at the wheels.

'The Lord George was praising the men to their face, till a messenger comes from the prince, and the Murray, Lord George I mean, cries out to McIvor, "See the prince commands me to leave nothing behind. Rather than leave one cannonball he will himself return. Did I not say at Derby that I would bring every man home but could not answer for the baggage? Yet am I not doing as much as any man might do?" "What occupation is this," cries the McIvor, "for Highland gentleman when they might cast off their plaids, and draw the claymore to repulse the redcoats?"

'Yet no man would yield the effort, or dishonour the command of their prince. We carried the cannonballs up the hill from the ford one by one, and loaded them back onto the carts. And Lord George orders sixpence for every man that would fetch till every ball was piled again on the carts. And as we went on Prince Charles himself came on foot for a time with the Colonel O'Sullivan to walk by the carts and give us good heart. Then the main column went on to Shap for the night with us coming behind. But we were sore weary and had to make camp near hand at Clifton, which was better than marching on or lying out for the rain had turned to snow.'

As if reliving that moment of exhaustion, Calum came to a halt, and breathed out deeply. Clementina poured a dram of whisky and reached it across. The storyteller drained it with one gulp, and resumed, determined to pay out every word to the end without pause.

'You will be understanding that on the way to Clifton we saw the cavalry riding two by two above us on the hill sounding drums and trumpets. McIvors and Glengarry men threw their plaids and ran to attack, but the enemy were afeared and fled, though Lord George was in the rage as he had not ordered a charge. Yet we followed them fleeing beyond the great House of Lowther which was closed against us. Evan Dhu and Calum went over the wall and caught hold of a man who told us that Cumberland himself was coming there with four thousand men.

'Cluny MacPherson ordered his men to come up now to McIvor and Glengarry. They ran like hounds to find us safely gathered to defend our walls against the redcoats. So the McIvor, Glengarry, his father's son, and Cluny were there waiting on Lord George's commands, when he, seeing that Cumberland would advance on Clifton, led the whole rearguard back. The redcoats are now one cannon's distance away, and we without cannon. A moon came over the clouds throwing its light.

'The Murray directs us to the left through a hedge, cutting thorns with our dirks, and then another hedge, till suddenly they were at us, dragoons on foot, armed to the teeth. Swords were drawn and we charged killing many, wounding and chasing them from the field like deer. But alas, Miss Flora, himself was at the front running on at them and Euan Dhu and myself with McIvor, when more redcoats come riding on the muir and surround us, striking with the sword. Calum is beaten to the ground, and Euan pierced, and the chief our father, shame to our blood and our name, is taken captive. But he was not wounded, I swear, since I saw it with my eyes lying on the ground. And Euan Dhu dead beside me, his blood still warm. You see we were too few to defend him. My own foster-brother, it is how he would have wished to die for McIvor, his chief, near at hand.'

Calum's eyes moved from Flora to Rose Bradwardine, as if he felt her gaze on his skin.

'It was Captain Waverley who came looking for us. He had seen our danger just when the moon was being covered once more with cloud. He pulled me back behind the hedge, blessings on his name and kindred, then he went to see if McIvor could be recovered. But we did not see him again. He was lost in the night but I do not think he was taken, for the redcoats had already left the Muir, sore from their loss. We could not stay to search in the darkness but marched back to Clifton. Cumberland was halted for a time and the prince went in safety to Carlisle. From there I left to bring dark tiding. The McIvors are marching with Glengarry till the prince comes home to his own in Scotland.

'My words are black and sad is their telling, but by God's grace the imprisoned will be released and the lost found. May the ancient right be restored for our eyes to see, and our ears to hear, and our tongues to acclaim.'

The story was done, with nothing omitted. The women sat in silence, looking into their own feelings. Calum bowed in acknowledgement and left the room.

From then frequent messages arrived each one hard on the heel of its forerunner. A garrison had been left in Carlisle. The prince was over the Border. The prince was at Douglas Castle, and then at Glasgow reviewing and resupplying the army. Carlisle had fallen to Cumberland, or was on the verge of surrender. Yet nothing carried the firsthand impact of Calum's recitation. None of the many words carried by successive detachments and couriers hurrying north added anything to the hard news that Fergus McIvor was unhurt but captured, and that Waverley was lost while presumed living. Calum himself headed onwards to Castle McIvor to prepare the clan for the worst, and to recoup his own strength.

Rose kept to her room, appearing red eyed to pick at food and quickly retiring to prayers and private sorrows. Flora kept her outward composure but felt frozen inside, unable to react to her own changed situation or respond to Rose's distress. As for Clementina, she brusquely attempted comfort, but could not hide the excitement which was driving her to energetic reorganisation of the household.

While the other two sat contained and pensive, her tall body was tensed in constant motion, driving on harassed servants, while she herself dragged out truckle beds, unfolded fresh bed linen and carried chairs from room to room in an effort to find more space. Downstairs the larder became a slaughterhouse as fresh meat and poultry was butchered from the dwindling winter stores of the surrounding farms.

The Jacobite army was expected daily and, in the continuing absence of her uncle, Clementina was determined to receive as many of the high command as Bannockburn House could hold, short of asking Flora and Rose to seek other lodgings. Never had the three young women seemed so divided by the circumstances that had first thrown them into each other's company and confidences.

On the third day of January, which was bitterly cold but dry, the bustle of preparations seemed to abate. Flora sat again by the fire in the back parlour and tried to imagine what Fergus would be feeling. The garrison at Carlisle had now definitely surrendered so it was likely that he had the company of fellow officers, perhaps in the dungeons of Carlisle Castle. What kind of place was that for an exhausted and hungry man? Yet while she felt a stab of worry, Flora acknowledged her brother's resilient strength. Even if he had been struck down on the battlefield a few days' rest could restore Fergus to health. But how was he to be freed?

Only Prince Charles could achieve that through a ransom or an exchange of prisoners. Surely that would be done, if perhaps she made a direct plea? Though Fergus was her brother, it was Charles with whom Flora had spent most of her younger years. In her mind Charles and Fergus were both family, almost brothers to one another. Carefully Flora nursed her thoughts, preparing inwardly for the prince's arrival.

The grey short lived day had already returned to dark when a rumble of wheels and hooves approached the front of the house. This was no backdoor messenger. Clementina rushed to the main hall ordering candles lit and the rarely opened doors pulled wide. Flora hung back on the curving stair at first floor level, from where she could look down unseen.

Three or four black cloaked figures came first clearing the way. Next two uniformed guards, pistols in hand, took up position on either side of the entrance. Then a much taller cloaked man was supported into the lighted hall. Behind crowded a gaggle of staff officers brushing off the frozen air with their coats and plaids. The prince drew himself to his full height, shaking off his bearers. They lifted the cloak from his shoulders revealing a richly brocaded dress uniform. The long once pudgy face had hardened, gaunt and grey. Clementina went down on her knee and kissed the prince's proffered hand. There was a quiet exchange, inaudible to Flora.

Clementina rose as if in invitation, but the prince stepped past her and leaning again on his attendants began a slow ascent of the stair. As the labouring threesome reached the first landing, Flora appeared in the shadows. Clementina was coming behind talking rapidly about rooms and suppers and fires. Charles came to a stop.

'So, my little Flora.'

'Your Highness.'

'Bad luck about Fergus. Damnable.'

'Can we offer –'

'Later. It's of a piece with the rest. Believe me.'

He looked round at Clementina, and she passed between them heading for the principal bed chamber. With a weary sigh Charles leaned again on his companions and began to drag himself and them along the passage. As a noisy wave of followers surged up the stairs behind him, Flora turned and hurried up the second narrow staircase to her own room.

3

AT THIS POINT a gap occurs in Flora McIvor's story, caused by the Jacobite defeat at Culloden, her brother's execution in Carlisle, and it would appear her own illness and grief. Yet there is a complication in the shape of Alister Ruadh McDonnell, Young Glengarry, who succeeded his father as chief a few years after these events The documents below – a testimony recorded from Chevalier O'Sullivan, an account sent by Flora herself to the prince's circle, and a letter from Clementina Walkinshaw to King James in Rome – only survive because they were found much later amidst Glengarry's own papers. He was informed of their contents and we surmise protected himself against them. They are copied here once more in a clumsy attempt to fill the silent years.

Colonel O'Sullivan

For myself take no heed. I sit easy at my table, honourable service given. None to carp or whinge. John William O'Sullivan, Colonel at your pleasure. As you may have heard, Major General to His Majesty the Prince, our own dear Tearlaigh, on the last expedition. My worth is known and my reputation needs no defending. A soldier born, now pensioned in Bella

Firenze. Friends call me Willie, and anyone who shares a bottle, earns the name. I call her Bella.

It is against Himself that calumny and vile insinuation aims. The Prince. They are lies, spread by those who should know better, those who never drew sword in the good cause, those who cling to old King James and descry his gallant son. But I was there, by Tearlaigh's right hand and saw it all before my eyes. You can rely on Willie. He was there, myself.

At Derby they all wanted to turn back for Scotland, every one of them, except himself. Tearlaigh was for London and no turning back, not a bit. But Murray, the estimable Murray, our General says there are three Hanoverian armies ready to close in and crush our Highlandmen. His Highlandmen, and ne'er a mention of the Irish Brigade, or the French, or even those poor English volunteers – a scrabble of untrained fellows, for we never saw the eyes of any Jacobite south of Carlisle. They didn't fancy our Scotch sauvages.
Anyroads, he raged and threatened and cajoled, the Prince, but he couldn't sway them. They were too far from hame. Was strange for he was their darling all the road south. Always on foot was Tearlaigh cracking with the men, wading through fords, walking by his horse to show he would go wherever they went, as long as they went with him. They said there was an army between us and London, not to mention Wade and Cumberland himself on each side. Yet Tearlaigh had the right, as now we know, there was no-one in London ready to fight, only to flee. So he might have been king, and us lording it at the Court of King Charlie.

Aye, but the truth is they never wanted that, those Highland chiefs, they wanted James Stuart, the Old Pretender so-called, back in Edinburgh as a Scottish king and them in their old style. They never drew a sword in England, not for Tearlaigh. Except at Clifton and then they were forced to the steel.

Mind it was a bad business. Right enough. Back we dragged ourselves through rain and snow, wagons stuck in the mud, swollen rivers, roads like an Irish bog. And Himself stayed in the coach and sulked. Always last up, he wouldn't move till the men were in order, and then they couldn't get moving for Himself. Still, he had cause, and we lost not a man, not till Carlisle anyway.

Aye, that was a business. We'd checked them at Clifton. Murray finally persuaded to fight, with Cluny MacPherson and McIvor to the fore. That was where McIvor was taken, in the dykes. And Waverley, the young English gallant, went to his aid, and he was cut off, lost somewhere in the north. Still it was his own country and he made it home after a time. Unlike McIvor.

We left a garrison at Carlisle to show we would be back. We had another army holding Scotland, and reinforcements landed from France. It was no rearguard action – Murray was wrong, as usual. We had to show it was tactical withdrawal, drawing them on to where our forces could regroup.

Cold, crabbed, Murray, looking down his aristocratic neb at John William O'Sullivan, Major-General. It was my decision to defend Carlisle against Wade or Cumberland, and Tearlaigh backed me. He was coming to himself a bit by then, after the shame of being overruled. He was seeing Murray now like another father, holding him back, undermining his authority, as his father had done.

Of course, Murray kept on north and Carlisle fell. It was a bad business, right enough. Cumberland refused all rule of war. Prisoners were executed, transported, starved, McIvor amongst them. He was hung like a common criminal, not exchanged like a gentleman officer. Fergus was a true Chief, of the old kind to be sure.

That was when I got to know, Flora, Miss McIvor, the Chief's sister. There was a lady if I ever saw one, and let me tell you, Willie has seen a few in his time, fine boned and dark haired with skin as white as an Irish dew. An exquisite flower. To Flora McIvor, life and good fortune. Whatever that fortune might be, for she had more than her share of troubles. But that's another tale for the telling.

Aye it was a business, but we came north to Stirling once more, after fleecing those tight fisted burgers of Glasgow. They had to shoe the whole army, at point of a sword, God damn them. They were all Hanoverians there, apart from the Walkinshaws and a few loyal families to be sure. But I am coming to that, our own Clementina, darling Clemmie. We'd better fetch another bottle, lest I say anything indiscreet. You know Willie, close as a Sligo whelk, even when drink is flowing.

That was when it all began, you see, Tearlaigh and Clementina. They'd been confidential before, in Edinburgh, but now it was doos cooing in the doocot. Sworn for life, swore Clementina later, whatever you need, whenever you call, I'll come winging to your breast. She loved the Court life, our Clemmie. Felt she belonged there amongst the intrigue and high living. That's not the life for Willie, no sir, a soldier born, pensioned here to the Tuscan sun. No Irish bogs for Willie, right enough.

She was a looker as well you see, not bonny and neat made like Flora. She was all height and style, fire in the eyes, hair piled back and nose in the air. But clever with it, she knew how to wheedle and coax and work round folk to her will, as I should know better than any. I suppose it's a kind of soldiering, the Court life with drills and manoeuvres, but not for the soldiering sort, no sir. She knew what she wanted, Clementina – Charlie. And she had him there just where she wanted him, and most of his staff to boot squeezed into the old Uncle's house at Bannockburn.

Tearlaigh, he took to it like a duck who hadn't seen water for a year. He just seemed to give way and lay there weak and pampered. It had all been too much for the overgrown laddie. We were dead beat after that retreat, right enough. Well, withdrawal for the time to be sure. Poor Flora moped and pined for McIvor, along with some other Scots lass who was weeping for young Waverley, till she was sent home to weep in her own tower. Clementina kept us entertained, in between tending His Majesty. We had no news from England, except that Cumberland was coming.

But he didn't come, not yet anyhow. Instead he sidelined cautious old Wade and sent Hawley instead. He was a dragoons man all set to put right the scandal at Prestonpans, when they ran with the rest. That was the first time, boyo, I saw the Highlanders charge and thanks to Our Lady I was behind them instead of before. Off go the plaids and sometimes the shoes as well till they're bare-arsed and working up to some kind of berserk fury. Those wailing pipes and the big swords banging on their shields as they caterwaul. Like a wave breaking o'er you in a sou'wester Kerry gale at full tilt. Nothing could stand in their way. Not Johnnie Cope and his empty coats anyhow. By God they ran like the devils of hell at their heels, which they were to be sure.

Now though it's Hawley for us, an iron discipline sort of fellow, in place of Wade or Cope. I suppose he's cashiered somewhere for his trouble. But for once Tearlaigh and Murray agreed on something. We should face down Hawley and move on Edinburgh. Suddenly everyone felt better, including Himself. We'd been leeching men since coming north – the sauvages would just take off on the notion, or arrive back as suited themselves. No conscript army here. Now everyone was fired upright enough and we advanced towards Falkirk, a kind of market town for cattle droving.

No sign of Hawley, or his army. Till we heard they were hanging around on the other side of Falkirk, not expecting to meet us anytime early. In truth Hawley was at his dinner in Callendar House where the good lady kept him chatting and eating at leisure. While we seized high ground above the town. So suddenly they saw their danger, snapping awake, and moved to block us, but it was too late. The rain was coming down fierce and chill and they were forced to climb up the hill to get at us with the wet in their eyes.

That should have been a rout, a greater triumph than the Pans, but something went wrong in the wind and rain. We couldn't see from one side to the other. Their left was swept aside but our left thought they were still coming on and moved back. Murray was the great general to be sure, but he threw it away. We could have destroyed them and taken Edinburgh again. We gave them a sore check whatever – Hawley smarted for it – but we had not won outright. Still it was another victory for a ragtag army that won at Edinburgh, Prestonpans, Clifton and now Falkirk. Let the chroniclers remember that and ponder. Yes, sir, John William O'Sullivan is no callow trooper but a seasoned campaigner, honourably retired. Your good health, sir.

Back to the doocots. Tearlaigh is at Bannockburn
House again, being cosseted by Clementina – the
returning warrior right enough. What can't he do now
that his fortune has turned? Truth to tell, it hadn't
been for turning since Derby and Himself was sunk
perpetually in gloom. Which made Her would-be
Leddyship all the more useful, though many named it
indulgence and spat from their cups. But Clementina
buoyed him up and fed his hopes, as I did myself,
for sure what had we else other than his hopes, our
Tearlaigh. Clementina and I understood that, which was
a kind of bond between us.

So, sir, consider, I ask you, my feelings when they
came that night with news of a secret Council. I should
explain that the Prince's Council had not met since
Derby. He would not have it, for he said it was a cabal to
deny his legitimate authority as Regent to his father, and
thwart his will as supreme commander. Which was the
bare black faced truth. Now they had met without him
and resolved on further retreat, back into the mountains
whence we had come, to be sure.

Secretary Broughton came to me with the paper, duly
signed by Murray and all the Chiefs remaining. But he
advised leaving the Prince till morning. Himself was
already in Clementina's embraces, and besides we both
knew the squall to come. That was the Broughton who
turned king's evidence and helped hang his old comrades.
Scotch duplicity at its worst. As I should know, right
enough. John William retired.

For Tearlaigh this new reverse was worse than Derby.
He replied formally, denying their case, as the record
shows, sir, but for him this was the end begun, and to
be sure, he was right once more. Even the retreat was

bungled by Murray who God knows it tried to blame the shambles on myself, Major-General O'Sullivan. They straggled off in disorder, leaving Tearlaigh and Murray still asleep. The last away were exposed to the guns of Stirling Castle and to cap all we blew up St Ninian's Kirk by accident. Aye, it was a damnable guddle, a fiasco right enough.

Now Murray and his crowd said they had secured the north for Tearlaigh, ready to fight another day. But Cumberland was ready for us now and came on with full supply. Culloden was waiting. We tried to fight on other ground, marching by night for a surprise attack, but time ran out. We fought with half an army, those who were not asleep in the ditches from hunger and exhaustion. We fought on the Butcher's slab and paid a heavy price.

The Prince refused to leave the field, courage undaunted to the last was Tearlaigh. Do not believe the lies, sir, I saw it with my own eyes. I was there, right enough. The horse was shot from under him amidst the slaughter, but he demanded another. We had to turn the horse's head and drag him from the scene. Himself was true. He did not cut and run there or the next day at Ruthven. The thing was finished and it was every man for himself, whatever the Highlanders claim. There was not another day for Scotland to restore her honour, nor ever has been. It was done with, as sure as I am sitting here today, John William O'Sullivan at your service. Aye, to be sure, I was there.

But listen now, if you think this an idle tale to spin out the afternoon, you have me wrong, sir, you don't have Willie's measure, right enough. You see we can't escape our own natures. We're born as we are and the tree grows straight or crooked. Each one turns out as they must be, king or commoner. If you don't believe an old soldier, look at Cumberland and Tearlaigh after Culloden. The Butcher is what they called this Prince of Hanover and butcher he proved name and nature, killing and burning without restraint or pity. Like some heathen savage, he laid the country waste. Another Cromwell to be sure.

But for Tearlaigh, it was his proudest moment. He was the young Prince again as on the march south, as if some dark cloud had lifted, some weary burden from his shoulders. He wandered on sea and mountain, hunted like a beast of the wild. A bad business you might say, but no thirst or hunger, not hot pursuit or near discovery, not cold rain or wind, could damp his spirit. Dressed in rags or in disguise, nothing could conceal that royal nature, generous and free. Though the price on his head was wealth beyond their dreaming, not a single Highlander betrayed him. Finally he was lifted off to a French ship, as I was myself, exhausted but victorious. He came a Prince and left as king of all their hearts, right enough.

To Tearlaigh, I say, our true Prince and to be King, Charles Edward Stuart. Your very good health, sir.

Yet it was a failure all the same. The French came too late. The English didn't rise. Just those damned bare shanked Highlanders. I call it an expedition, for there was no campaign, no army to speak of. Only his spirit carried the day. And Europe saluted the gallant Prince. As I do, sir, to this day and hour, and every hour left to me beneath the sun.

Yes, so what next, you may wonder? The intrigue, the politics, the backstairs business. Not a soldier's work. But I was left with Clementina in my care, and Flora McIvor after a time. Herself escaped Scotland first to support the cause, whatever might come of it, and then she sent for Flora. But Paris was too hot and we regrouped in Boulogne, waiting the call. But it didn't come. A bad business.

We had to make shift for ourselves; that was the truth of it right enough. Tearlaigh himself was bundled out of Paris when the Peace was signed; they didn't want him around disturbing their precious peace. So he went into the dark, incognito, leaving us to do as we might. Until, well, that is another story altogether. John William will not tangle with her again. No, sir, my troth is pledged to Bella.

We got embroiled in English business in Boulogne. And Glengarry arrived. Young Glengarry, but he was the elder son, you know. Enough said. It was not soldier's business, not at all. Better leave it for today. Enough said, but never trust a Highland Chief. I learned the hard way. Believe me, I was there, John William O'Sullivan saw it with his own eyes. Rum business, Tearlaigh sent for her eventually, his true love right enough. Still, less said, sooner and so forth.

Tomorrow the sun will shine again. I am a soldier by profession. My pleasure, sir, I served my Prince without regret. I've earned my place. Don't believe the lies. Indeed, not at all, I was there. Your good health, and mine to be sure. John William retired. Yes, our health, right enough.

Flora McIvor

Young Glengarry is a traitor. I swear in peril of my soul that what I write is true, and beg loyal servants of the House of Stuart to take warning. This man of noble blood and reputation is false, a despiser of virtue. Young Glengarry, elder son of McDonell, Chief of Glengarry, has used the lineage and honour of his name to betray our cause.

I am writing this in sickness and in sorrow, but in full possession of my mind and pen. I beg you who read, conscious of my family's own service, to believe what is written here and take warning, for all our sakes.

There is no enmity between McIvors and McDonells. Our houses are related by kin and marriage, without any ancient feud. I bear no grudge or prejudice. I was brought up by my parents to respect all those of the name McDonell. When I was under the protection of Clementina Sobieski, I heard the Chiefs of Glengarry praised for their loyalty to the true line and for their Catholic faith.

The grandfather of Young Glengarry, Alister Dubh McDonell, led the clan at Killiecrankie and at Sheriffmuir. In that first battle he lost his brother, Donald Gorm, and at the second, his kinsman Clanranald fell by his side. Though of advanced years, Alister Dubh cast his bonnet in the air shouting 'Revenge today but lament tomorrow'. Then he led the charge that gained one side of the field. This is what I heard as a child.

Some say that McDonells have never lost lands or position on account of their loyalty. By keeping friends on both sides they avoid the fate of others. But it is the duty of chiefs to look after their people by holding the land for the good of all. It is different for each clan according to their neighbours and kin. McDonell kept his oldest son in France while the clan went out led by his younger son, Aeneas, and his cousin Lochgarry. The McDonells fought courageously till Aeneas' death sent them home from Falkirk. Due to the early loss of our parents, we could only commit Clan McIvor body and soul to the Rising.

After the expedition was underway, Young Glengarry sailed from France, where he was serving in the army, with reinforcements and supplies. But they were caught at sea, and he was imprisoned in London till the affair came to its desperate end.

I was sheltered after Culloden by the remnant of my clan. Due to the kindness of Edward Waverley, my poor people were saved the worst excesses of the Butcher Cumberland. However I was not reconciled to a life of concealment at Castle McIvor. Fergus had left no heirs, so was I not his successor?

Though captured in open fight, Fergus was treated as a common criminal and we were not allowed to bring his body home to rest amongst his kin. Nor was I permitted to visit him before the execution. But I know that he died as bravely as he lived, and I was resolved to continue the struggle. I wanted to follow his example in the cause of McIvor, not to be a retired gentlewoman dependent on others, or a religious. Fergus' death would be avenged.

I received a message from Clementina Walkinshaw, urging me to come to France. This letter was delivered by the hand of a McDonell clansman. I was to join a party of loyal Jacobites that had gathered to strike another blow, this time in England. I found Clementina at Boulogne, where other sympathisers including Colonel O'Sullivan were gathered. Young Glengarry was of their number, though when I arrived he was in England preparing this new assault.

When Alister Ruadh returned, he insisted on the strength of our connection that he should be my personal protector. Our relationship grew close, and he proposed that we should marry when things were more settled. I agreed to this as an honourable alliance for the daughter of McIvor.

Glengarry was our leader. Elegant, tall, domineering; he had the capacity to command and inspire. We were all in some sense under his spell, but I more than others. In my grief and anger I saw him as the instrument of our revenge. He could inflict harm on those who had so brutally and effectively destroyed us. Or so he persuaded me. I was drawn by that conviction to his side, his service. Where Charles Edward had failed he could succeed.

I am writing frankly to prove that I am honest, and to prevent others from discrediting my name. It was a time of war and we were a clandestine force, designing to overthrow a complacent enemy from within.

There were two sides to our hidden endeavours. In London a party led by Murray of Elibank planned to kidnap members of the royal family as a signal for English Jacobites to rise. At the same time the loyal Highland clans would break the chains which bound them after Culloden. The messenger between these parties was Glengarry, and we were assured by him that Prince Charles had given assent to our actions.

Delays were reported, but we had no suspicion of Alister Ruadh. He was the moving spirit, keeping us in thrall. Cut off in Boulogne we had few other sources of information. Rumours spread that blame for our setbacks lay with Clementina Walkinshaw. Not only was she close to Charles Edward, but her sister was lady in waiting at the Court in London. I knew this was wrong – none has been truer to the cause than Clementina. All this time Glengarry was undermining the venture while pretending to be its mainspring.

The action in London did not take place. Twice I went to England with Glengarry, providing cover for his travels as the well born Highland wife. The plan was to strike that blow against the Hanoverian dynasty in their own palace in London. These visits were taken up by inconclusive rumours, and muddled assignations with Jacobite sympathisers. We stayed openly in prosperous inns, which Glengarry said would avert suspicion. He was always in funds.

From these visits I learned that Prince Charles himself had been in London consulting his supporters and inspecting the defences of the Tower. He had even pledged to change his religion in order to win over the English Protestants. But abduction and assassination should have given me pause. If Charles had granted permission, then disappointment had changed his nature.

Glengarry did not divulge his inner calculation, or what progress was being made. Perhaps because there was none – none at any rate favourable to the Stuart cause. Alister Ruadh was accomplished at being importantly secret, of knowing things too risky to share. Meanwhile he spent his time between assignations resting and enjoying the comforts of city life. Did he take delight in his own cleverness, his deceit?

Likely it had been all along a trap for the plotters, flushing out the actively disloyal while putting off moderate sympathisers. Murray of Elibank appeared beside himself, fixing everyone with piercing stares while boasting of what explosives would achieve. The gamble of a reckless few were cruelly exploited with a double hand. Cold malice, even while I shared his bed and table.

The renewed campaign in Scotland was also betrayed, still born. The brave and honest Archibald Cameron, Lochiel's own brother, was seized. O'Sullivan told me that Dr Archibald stood accused of using the French money concealed at Loch Arkaig for his own selfish purpose. The accuser was Young Glengarry. This became the means by which the whole failure in Scotland could be blamed on someone else. It did not ring true even as I heard the insinuations. Dr Cameron was a man of principal and soul, as he later proved on the scaffold.

When O'Sullivan had gone I looked about the narrow rooms which Glengarry rented in Boulogne. It was an old house with wide chimneys, twisting stairs and panelling blackened by centuries of smoke. I had seen Alister Ruadh handle papers from a wooden chest, and found it beneath the window seat. Below the panel below was set forward, leaving a hidden chamber behind. Now I had my hand on the matter. I took a short sword and broke the lock and chain.

I was trembling as I laid out the contents – folded letters, rolled papers, lists and maps. Yet I sat through the night reading by candlelight. There was correspondence from and to London, Scotland, Rome, and His Royal Highness Charles Edward. Some were in cipher, mainly letters for the Duke of Newcastle in the English Government. But the code was also in the chest with numbers substituted for names and places. Glengarry himself used the name Peregrine, Peregrine Pickle, a supposed hero of Romance. It was bizarre and even laughable, were the effect not so deadly.

Everything had been laid bare from the start, everything that was planned in London and Scotland. Even the list of clans pledged to rise, with the numbers each could bring again to the field, had been passed on to Newcastle. This had been gathered by Glengarry's own cousin but that had not prevented its exposure. This was treason dark and near.

As my mind slowed, I felt an icy chill creep around my heart. Pickle had sent Archibald Cameron to his death. And here was a letter written by Glengarry to

King James' secretary in Rome, accusing Dr Cameron of using the Loch Arkaig Louis d'Or for his own purposes. At the same time the writer pled his own loyalty and usefulness. In these last months it had been Glengarry who had been able to travel widely, and to keep these rooms in which I sat. In the kist was a small bag of gold coins – Louis d'Or.

The ashes had died in a cold grey dawn before my mind turned to what I could do. My pulse began to race again but this time with fear. Clementina had been called away to Charles' royal presence. O'Sullivan and others were still around me in Boulogne, but in whom can I confide? Everyone here is linked to Glengarry. What if he returns to find his secret papers disturbed? I replaced them as best I could and hid everything again behind the hollow panel.

A few days later, revolving everything constantly in my brain without rest, I have sat down once again in this fearful room and written my account. I am sending it to a name and holding address that I saw used by Glengarry for correspondence with His Royal Highness, Prince Charles. Forgive me if I have done wrong, but I have no other person to whom I can turn to prevent further treachery. What further harm? Before more lives are lost.

I continue feverish and anxious. I beg Charles' advisers and trusted friends to read these words and credit me. I cannot find rest before committing them to your care. If Clementina is at hand, she can vouch for my faith and honesty. I am no Peregrine, false in name and nature.

I bear no spite at Alister Ruadh for dishonouring me and the name of McIvor. God will see justice done for such pitiless wrong. But I charge Glengarry as a black traitor, a twice deceiver. He is a child of Satan who looks and speaks fair, while devising mischief. This place is haunted by his poisoned secrets. I must leave these rooms and never return.

Please believe me, and act for the best,
Your servant,
Flora McIvor

Clementina Walkinshaw

Sir, I write to you as a faithful servant of the House of Stuart, Clementina, younger daughter of the late Chevalier John Walkinshaw, and niece of Sir Hugh Paterson of Bannockburn.

The service of my family to the good cause is well known, both in the late expedition of Prince Charles Edward to Britain, but also long since in the assistance rendered by my father to the household of King James, and in particular to her late Majesty Clementina Sobieski, whose rescue he attended bringing Her Majesty across Europe to His Majesty at Court. It is for Queen Clementina that I was named.

My purpose in writing is to plead the cause and the necessity of Miss Flora of the House of McIvor in Scotland, sister to the late Chief Fergus McIvor who was executed in England for his part in the invasion of 1745. She as you will know was a child in ward of the Court of King James in Rome, and later in the service of Queen Clementina who provided in her will for Miss McIvor's education by the Sisters of St Teresa of Avila, until her return to Scotland to join the household of her brother.

In representing Miss McIvor's situation, and her claim on the attention, through your good offices

of His Gracious Majesty King James, and of His
Grace the Cardinal Prince Henry Stuart, I wish to
acknowledge openly my own position and to correct the
misrepresentations and calumnies that have been spread
by my enemies and by those who have sought to belittle
Prince Charles Edward in his father's eyes.

During the expedition led by the Prince as Regent in
Britain, I attended the royal Court in Scotland and was
honoured to receive the trust and favour of His Royal
Highness. At that time, and in my own home country,
I pledged my undying loyalty and love to the Prince.
Subsequently, after the failure of the expedition, through
no fault of the Regent who showed undaunted courage,
I continued my service in exile in Europe. When I was
summoned by His Royal Highness to accompany him in
his lonely travails following his expulsion from France,
I readily came to his side where I have remained since.
I make no claim on the Prince's person but continue
faithful to the love I pledged, at His good pleasure.

Miss McIvor, as you know, was also in attendance at
the Regent's Court in Scotland, and an active supporter
of the Prince's army through the participation of Clan
McIvor which provided three hundred clansmen led
by the Chief. He was captured at the battle of Clifton
leading an action against Cumberland's dragoons and
subsequently hanged at Carlisle. The estate is forfeit
though some of the clan remain living on their lands.
After the cruel suppression of the Highlands of Scotland,
Miss McIvor joined a group of exiles in Boulogne where
she was for a time in my company along with others
committed to continuing the struggle in Britain.

The plan for a further Rising in both England
and Scotland has been regarded by some as a rash
undertaking, yet it was the failure of England to

participate that caused the retreat of 1745. Loyal supporters in England have been untouched by the destruction in Scotland, despite which the clans were once more ready to fight for their ancient rights.

This plan was betrayed, as is well known throughout Europe. But some have alleged, as you must be aware, that this treachery was at my instigation, due to my connection with the Court of Hanover in London through my elder sister Catherine. This a baseless lie, and I have accordingly attached a deposition begun by Miss McIvor regarding Alister Ruadh of Glengarry, now styled Chief of Glengarry, but commonly known as Young Glengarry.

Though containing distressing matter, and showing signs of distress or fever, this is an account of grave importance which will I believe not have come to your hand by any other party. The witness made by Miss McIvor supports my own account of these matters in which we were both closely involved. I fear that Miss McIvor's testimony has not been believed, or set aside due to its personal nature, and that Glengarry remains a danger to all those attached to our cause.

At the time of her writing, Flora McIvor was sick and in great trouble in Boulogne. I was able to secure her temporary relief through the good offices of the Sisters of Teresa, and she has been recovering in their Convent at Paris. I give thanks that God in his mercy has spared dear Flora for the salvation of her soul, for she is as I am a faithful daughter of the Church. It is my sincere plea that His Majesty King James, and His Grace the Cardinal Prince Henry, provide some succour to their daughter in distress, mindful of her close connection with their family, and her devoted service.

Our dear Flora has suffered both as a faithful servant

and as a true Highlander. Her betrayal at the hands of Glengarry is a grievous personal wound, striking at the heart of everything she grew to value as the daughter and sister of McIvor, whose unswerving devotion to the House of Stuart has been the animating principle of their lives. I beg that you prevent that wound from becoming mortal.

I trust that you will accept my good faith in writing in this matter, and my obligation to His Majesty King James. You will know that I have borne a child to Prince Charles Edward. She has been baptised Louisa as a daughter of the Church and of the House of Stuart. It is my concern that Louisa should be brought up in accordance with her station, and her importance in present circumstances to the continuation of the royal line.

But, in confidence, the situation of His Royal Highness Prince Charles does not allow for his daughter's upbringing. Living as a fugitive, in constant disguise from spies or assassins, has made Charles Edward suspicious and dark in temperament. His former generosity is cankered by mean imaginings. He seeks ever more demeaning incognitos and salves his disappointments with wines and strong spirits. Moreover he has abandoned the practice of our religion, proclaiming himself Protestant.

I confess that I am sometimes in fear for the safety of my person and of our child. I beg that you bring these matters also to the attention of His majesty King James, and that I may continue in communication with yourself until some remedy can be found for these ills.

I am the faithful servant of His Majesty,
Clementina Walkinshaw

4

FLORA SAT NEAR the high window to make the most of what light was available. The aperture was barred on the other side of the glass, but a wan sun still warmed her hands as they moved over the texture of the cloth keeping pace with her immaculate stitching. It appeared, to her surprise, this early girlhood skill had survived her sickness. Flora felt a weakening tremor of relief wash through her. This was something at least for which she could practice gratitude.

It was Sister Teresa who had coaxed her back to the needle, providing threads and a sample of embroidered cloth from a shop in the Rue de Théâtre. Or so she had said, amidst many other tempting descriptions of life beyond the narrow wooden bed on which Flora had lain for longer than she could remember or measure. Boulogne seemed as remote as a past life. And before that.

Coming gradually out of her fever, Flora had been determined to accumulate papers and to write. Again the Sister had provided, laying out pen, ink and paper. But the astute nurse quickly sensed that some other distraction was necessary to her patient's recovery. Pulling herself onto a stiff backed chair Flora would sort pages into shifting piles. Then she covered sheet after sheet with scribbled journals, day after day relapsing into exhausted dream-troubled sleep, when eased back onto the bed. Then the sorting would begin once more.

The little room was as restricted as a cell. The barred window closed off one end and a solid door the other. Between the bed and a plain table there was just enough space for the chair. So Flora preferred now to put the chair between the table and the window with its back to the wall. Under the table was a basket piled high with papers. They were unevenly stacked but Flora knew that each one was covered with her writing. She wanted to leave them there for now and trust to the steady motion of her hands slipping in the needle, tucking the cloth and pulling through in supple sequence. It was safe and calm to sew while ignoring the scribbled journals.

But Flora was not yet able to leave them alone. They were in her mind and on the beating of her pulse. Sometimes it had seemed as if that beat would possess her by completely overwhelming her thoughts. Perhaps she should burn the sheets page by page. There was a tiny fireplace between the table and the door. No fire had been lit in its cold grate since Flora had occupied this cell. Yet she had a candle at night, shaded by a linen cover.

If only she had been able to sit by Fergus's bed and light a candle. To watch with his body through the hours of darkness, before laying him in the friendly earth of McIvor. Tonight, she thought, I shall light a candle for Fergus. She could go to chapel with Sister Teresa. The immortal soul outlived the body. Did it lie in some common grave twisted, broken, unwashed?

Her left hand had pulled a paper from the basket. The fabric she was sewing rested on her knee below the sheet which was covered in jagged letters. Poor stitching. Her eyes wandered for a moment as the marks came into focus. Read what had been written. For the first time. Flora swithered.

'When I was thirteen years old I heard a voice in my father's garden at Donremy. It came from the side where the church stood, and was followed by a bright light. At first I was frightened, but presently I became aware that it was the voice of an angel, who has ever since been my guide and instructor. It was St Michael. I also saw St Catherine and St Margaret, who admonished me and directed me. I could easily distinguish by the voice whether it was an angel or a saint that spoke to me. They are usually accompanied by a bright light. The voices are soft and sweet. The angels appeared to me with natural heads. I have seen them and do see them with my eyes.'

Flora was standing reciting these words, learned by heart. Was it her mother in France long since, or Clementina in Rome? Her lesson. Her performance for special occasions. She had no need of the paper, even now. 'Since then I have done nothing except in conformity with these voices and revelations. And now, during my trial, I speak only as they prompt me.'

When she was eighteen, the voice had told her to go Vaucouleurs where she would find a captain to take her to the king of France. So the Maid of France became an emblem of war, mounted and armoured against the English. Till at the siege the voice foretold the capture of the city and the wounding of the Maid by an arrow penetrating six inches into her shoulder.

All of her life Flora had prepared for the call to arms in a holy cause. She had become an orphan in the faith. And when the call came, she had repulsed the plea of Edward Waverley for domestic happiness. But unlike the Maid of Orleans she had not been allowed to fight. It was Fergus who had been captured, tried and hung. Only then had Flora tried to strike her own blow. The Maid had been burned but not dishonoured or shamed. She put the paper to one side without reading any further.

Her hands remembered twisting white cockades on the huge rough board table in Castle McIvor. They moved gently over her lap without disturbing the present piece of work. That had been the time of hope, her emblem of war. Then the occupation of Edinburgh and victory at Prestonpans, with Fergus at the centre of the triumph. Supported by Flora, who fussed over her clansmen as family. And all had revolved like a courtly dance around Charles Edward.

But after the army had gone south she felt discarded and useless, cooped up at Bannockburn House waiting. At least Clementina had known how to take command. Was that why she had obeyed the younger woman's summons and gone to Boulogne? She wanted to strike her own blow, even though Scotland seemed for now without hope.

Could such violence deliver a just return? Yet Flora had gone along with it. Extreme violence had been visited on her Highland people, on her brother by the House of Hanover. She wanted to reply in kind. Now she doubted her own self. Who had participated in that wild scheme? Was it some other Flora who had been blind to Glengarry's double dealing, to the hopelessness of those hidden devisings?

It was a black maze from which you could not escape whole, as had always been intended. But worse the purpose was wrong; no good could come from such moral blindness. Why had she not realised what now she saw? Already she had been sick, deluded. Beautiful treacherous Glengarry had appeared as her protector, a guardian angel amidst distress. She had fallen under his malign spell. To be resisted.

Flora looked at the embroidery beneath her hand.

The image was of Mount Carmel, which Sister Teresa had brought unfinished from a linen store to distract her patient. In the last week or two, after she had begun to get up from bed in the mornings, Flora had dressed herself in a plain smock provided by the Sisters. It hung loosely around her slight figure, but she had been able to go for meals to the Sisters' bare refectory. Only the household nuns and other lay attendants were there, since in this Carmelite house many were secluded for solitary meditation. Silence was the mealtime rule, but there was also a reading taken from some improving work, often the writings of St Teresa the founder. It felt like some kind of progress.

Even in her weakened state Flora's ear was acute. She heard a difference between the Saint's polished exhortations, her 'Way of Perfection', and rawer passages from St Teresa's 'Life'. They spoke of conflict and a never ending struggle to gain recognition, without casting off obedience to the Church. Everyone around the young Teresa was consumed by their sense of honour, and the desire to avoid shame.

Something in this rang true. The shame which people feared arose from race, birth, sex, religious standing. No-one was free of taint, least of all a young woman who despite her family's Jewish origins was determined to reform the Church. But Teresa repudiated honour and shame. She fought with weapons of faith and love, yet she too had been sorely wounded by her weapons, pierced like Jeanne d'Arc.

Flora's attention strayed back towards the basket of papers. But instead she raised the needle and began to sew. It was enough for the day. Her arm rose and fell with the soothing movement of thread, up and through like an incoming tide. She felt as if her fight was over. Perhaps dreams would leave her sleeping self in peace.

The next morning Flora rose early after an undisturbed rest. She felt stronger. After the morning meal she took a brush to help sweep the refectory. Then the long wooden tables were washed and scrubbed. She saw Sister Teresa nodding her encouragement, while still observing the rule of silence.

Back in her own room, Flora looked for a moment at her embroidery and then moved her chair round between the table and the bed. Next she lifted the basket of jumbled papers from under the table onto its working surface. She sat down and pushed the sewing to one side. The time had come to read and sift, to recover that time. Flora pushed back her hair that had grown long. It would need to be tied back if such a thing as a ribbon could be found in this place.

She did not begin with the top leaf. Rather Flora pulled a page at random from the foot of the pile. It was headed, 'my own Alister Ruadh'. She shoved it back. Another sheet was pulled out. It was prefaced as 'Lives of Martha and Mary'. But the following page was urgently scribbled with references to 'Rose' and 'Clementina', heavily scored out and replaced with 'Martha', and 'The Magdalene' and 'Mary, Mother of Christ'.

When had Flora last read from the Gospels? She glanced round and noticed that her well worn Douai Bible had been placed beneath the pillow. Sister Teresa had been her guardian angel over these restless, fevered weeks. But this much scored sheet made no sense, not now at any rate. She began to glance through the pages one after another. Some sections were descriptions of things that happened in Boulogne or London. But these short passages gave way to longer incoherent passages which mixed the three friends – Flora, Clementina and Rose – with characters from history, religion or legend. It was like her girlhood library regurgitated, with every volume mixed into the next.

Yet leaning back against the chair back, Flora could see that the overall intent was a battle with shame, like Teresa's. There was shame in her giving way to Glengarry's promises of marriage. There was shame in Clementina's liaison with O'Sullivan, and her pregnancy. Shame even in Rose's abject dependence on Waverley's goodwill. The codes of honour had been disrupted, breached, by the strange circumstance of war and exile. Was she still bound by them, or could she leave that shame behind her?

Her mind turned to Clementina's first child. It had seemed imperative that Charles Edward should not know of this birth, since she was in some fashion pledged to the prince. Her condition had prevented any travel to London in the Elibank affair. The secret was even more pressing now that Clementina had gone to Charles. Would O'Sullivan blab? He had been the reluctant messenger, sent to fetch the Magdalene. But by this time the baby had been given to the nuns in Boulogne, and the whole affair cloaked in silence. Clementina was now mother to Charles' own daughter Louisa. Was that not cause for shame? And Flora was party to it.

But Clementina acknowledged no shame. Even as Rose had gone to Waverley in search of an honourable marriage – something retrieved from the wreckage – this friend had chosen to live beyond convention. She openly claimed her devotion to Charles. As for O' Sullivan, he had been shrugged off as a passing convenience – for both parties. Clementina considered herself on active service, and claimed the freedoms of a man in her situation. Who was Flora to deny that right? The conventions of Palazzo

Muti had not equipped her for what followed. She could not go back to the thirteen year old Flora at Clementina Sobieski's side. Neither innocence nor certainty could be regained.

There was a gentle tap on the door. Flora came to herself, suddenly unsure how long she had been lost in her memories. Sister Teresa came in and sat on the bed.

'You are looking well today, Flora.'

'I feel much better, Sister.'

'Sister Maria asked if you might be able to help her in the mornings with the bedding.'

'Of course, I am sure I could do that now.'

'These are not hands that were bred to laundry though.' Teresa reached across and took one of Flora's slender hands in her own which though fine boned were roughened by age and labour. 'You have had a difficult time.'

'Did I say much in my fevers?' Flora glanced uneasily towards the papers beside her on the table.

'Not during the night. I think you wrote it all instead, when you were calmer in the daytimes.' Teresa took a breath. 'Mother Abbess understands something of your history, if not everything that has taken place since the war in Britain. She wants you to consider remaining here for a longer time.'

Flora's question was in her look.

'Yes, perhaps to seek a vocation.'

'And what of those pages?'

'That is between you and a confessor, Flora. War is not kind to women. They are always among the victims.'

'Please thank Mother Abbess for me, Teresa. I know you have all been very kind to me.'

'But?' Teresa's lined face seemed faded and grey as it bent towards Flora's delicate oval face and luminous white skin. The eyes were enlightened, kind.

'I will think about what Mother Abbess suggests,' Flora deferred.

'But perhaps you are not ready for the enclosed life?'

It was observation more than question, so Flora let it lie.

'I deal with our community's business in the town.' Teresa took up her own thought. 'There is a shop close by in Jean St Denis that takes in fine needlework. Its owner is a Madame Guyon who is a widow. She might be able to employ your skills, while you decide what to do.'

'Yes, I would like that,' responded Flora immediately.

'Good, I will speak to her when I am out next. In the meantime, don't overtax your strength, or be anxious. God cares for each of his daughters.' And with a reassuring smile the older woman returned to her duties.

Flora sat as she had been before, and wondered at her lack of hesitation. To become a seamstress. But it would be living by her own hands. She gathered up the scribbled pages and put them back into the basket below her table. It was time to find Sister Maria and do some washing. Her arms stretched in readiness right down to her finger tips.

She was on a river. The boat was moving of its own accord and black water parted on each side of the prow. Thick weeds waved below the surface. The banks on each side were covered by bushes or reeds.

She stared down and trailed her arms in the current. She was searching for pieces from the river. Trawling them from the flow. They were laid out behind her in the bottom of the boat. But something was missing. It was the most important.

Beneath water was speeding up. She was being pursued. As the boat raced she saw something deep below and reached out. It was slipping through her fingers. A face turned. His head was on the river bed. She could not reach.

Hair like weeds, pale flesh, empty eyes. She was falling.

Flora sat up, awake. Her pulse was racing. There was a dull grey light at the window. She wiped her forehead on the sheet, got up and sat at the table. She reached below for paper and dipping her pen began to write rapidly describing her dream.

Then her hand slowed and she put the pen down. This dream had occurred before, though not in recent days. It was already recorded somewhere in her accumulated pages. And she knew the story she was in. Isis searching for her brother, his dismembered body. That was the real sorrow beneath everything. Which she would take with her from the convent as she had brought it there.

Quietly she lifted her unlit candle and opened the door of her room. The corridor stretched in both directions passed repeated doors. A night light flickered on a little table at each end. Flora stepped along quietly and lit her candle from the flame. Then she returned to her room sheltering the candle with her hand.

She set the holder down and lifted the whole basket of papers onto the table beside it. Then carefully without reading any of the words on them she burnt the pages one by one. Till all that she had was a basketful of ashes. By the time she had finished the light outside was brighter than the solitary candle. She shivered, blew the candle out and got back beneath her bedcovers. Quickly she slipped below the surface into peaceful sleep.

Flora's apprenticeship came in trial stages. First she received piece work from Madame Guyon, which she was allowed to complete in the privacy of her own room. Teresa brought the packages which Sister Maria carried along to the seamstress, with a bustle of advice. More housekeeper than nun, Maria was diverted by this unexpected turn of events and full of advice and critical comment, as the bundles were unwrapped and then repackaged for return to the shop.

The work was straightforward. It involved hemming and alterations to the stomachers and underskirts which supported the elaborate dresses of fashionable women. 'How could anyone fit in that?' scolded the buxom Maria. Flora noticed wryly that she had not been entrusted with the visible silks and satins. Perhaps Madame Guyon and Teresa had agreed that these were unfit for import to the convent. She progressed steadily and efficiently with these routine tasks, finishing ahead of whatever schedule Madame Guyon observed.

Whether Flora had passed her first test, or the delivery routine was proving too cumbersome, Sister Teresa announced that Mother Abbess had given permission for the apprentice to leave her house and go to the shop by day coming back each evening. This was a notable concession for an enclosed order and suggested that the hope Flora might stay on in the convent had been surrendered. The new arrangement would begin on the next Monday.

On Sunday evening, when the house was already falling into the even deeper silence that presaged sleep, there was a muffled tap at Flora's door. There was Sister Maria casting hurried glances up and down the corridor, while holding a cloth cover tightly over a tray.

'Sister, come in.'

'Thank you, Flora, thank you kindly. What a lovely name that is. Flora, the flower, so Teresa tells me with all her learning. I have little enough of that I fear.'

'Have you brought me more work?'

'No, not at all.' Maria's voice sank. 'I thought we should

trim your hair before, you know, you are out and about in the town.' And she uncovered her tray to reveal scissors, a comb and brush, and a little wooden framed mirror.'

'A mirror!'

'Hush now or Mother Abbess will be down on us.'

With deft though pudgy hands, Maria set out her utensils on the little table. She pulled the table round against its long side and gestured for Flora to sit before the propped up mirror. She lit an extra candle. Then taking up the long dark waves of hair she clipped them short against the head, side and back. The shorter strands crimped and curled naturally.

'This is how Parisian woman wear their hair,' Maria pronounced firmly.

'But I am a seamstress,' laughed Flora, 'not a lady of fashion.'

'Working for fashionable women,' insisted Maria. 'We can't have you wandering around like Delilah before Samson trimmed her locks, or was it the other way round? I always nod off at Scripture reading.'

'Maria, it is lovely. I can't thank you enough.' Flora looked at her image in the mirror, surprised that the likeness was so unchanged from what she remembered.

'Oh dear but I'll miss you, Flora, amongst us dried out old sticks.'

'Oh Maria, don't cry. Who knows whether I'll manage at all?'

'Don't be daft. Of course you'll manage. These are the cleverest little hands I have ever seen.'

She gave the delicate hands a squeeze and busied herself tidying the tray. Then she bent down breathlessly to gather up Flora's abundant shed locks.

'Don't, Maria, please let me tidy those.'

'No. Miss Flora, don't you, please. Let me wait on you

properly, just this once. I never met a Jacobite lady before, yet we pray daily for the restoration of King James. Did you meet Bonnie Prince Charlie?'

'I did, Maria.'

'Is he as handsome as they say?'

'He was, Maria, when he was young. I knew him then in Rome.'

'I thought so, I did. Who was this Flora MacDonald in Scotland?'

'Maria!'

'Don't mind an old stout lady, Miss. We all have our dreams.'

Flora gathered the kindly figure in her arms and hugged as hard as she could. 'Thank you, dear Maria. I could not have got through without you and Teresa. Thank you for my hair cut. I'll hold up my head in Paris now.'

'Good night,' whispered Maria as she inched the door open and squeezed out. 'God bless and sleep tight.'

Flora was left smiling to herself in the narrow room. She lifted up her hands to feel the new shape that her head had been given. Then she pulled out her own clothes from under the bed in search of the plainest dress she could find.

The Carmelite convent of St Teresa was sightless from outside. Its only windows looked inwards onto a narrow courtyard and few sounds seemed to penetrate, even though the building was in the centre of Paris. When she emerged on the first morning and looked about, Flora could see why. The little street onto which the gates opened was blocked beside the convent by a wall which screened the Louvre Palace. So the long external wall adjoined the quiet courts in front of the Palace. On the other side the Convent was built against a spacious Oratory with its monastic house and church. St Teresa had walled her in silence.

By contrast turning at the other end of the street into the Rue St Honoré, Flora was met by a barrage of noise. She shrank back putting hands to her ears, as carts, carriages, horses, barrows, hawkers and hucksters fought for space. After a few moments she launched herself into the throng and was carried along with its current. She had only yards to overcome as St Jean Denis was the third street along, past the Church of St Honoré. It was a narrow street full of shops but she had no difficulty finding her new place of employment.

Madame Guyon was presiding in the front shop. She was a stately figure, tall and dressed from head to toe in black satins. Her features were broad, olive-skinned and impassive.

'Miss Maceevour, you are welcome to my house.'

'No, please, call me Flora.'

'Well, Miss Flora, you are welcome.'

'Thank you, I hope my work will be satisfactory.'

'Very, I am sure. Now please come to the work table.'

There was something in Madame's speech that Flora could not place, but there was no time for further conversation. Behind the small front shop was a long room stretching to the back of the building. On one side was a wide extended bench for cutting and sewing. In every other direction garments hung or were draped from a variety of hooks, rods, improvised pulleys and poles. Two other women were already busy at the table.

Flora's piece work on plain undergarments had not prepared her for the visual splendours of the workroom. The robes, dresses and coats which festooned Madame Guyon's establishment were of the richest and most elaborate kind. Some were clearly court costumes while others represented the wealth and leisure of the city. Moreover the garments were for men and women. She raised a hand and drew her palm down over the layered flounces of a mantua. It reminded her of the dresses that had hung on in Clementina Sobieski's wardrobe long after the Queen's death.

'Good fabric,' Madame Guyon noted with approval, 'but old fashioned now for general wear.'

This was a changed world from the Convent of St Teresa three streets away. Flora could see why her tasks there had been so restricted. Soon she was seated at the table and being shown her first jobs by the two women who were called Jeanne and Adrienne. Madame Guyon returned to her role as public ambassador. The day passed quickly. Flora was quick to learn and the others were glad to see another ready pair of hands. There seemed to be no end of jobs finished, half-finished and still to be done. Flora hurried home through the darkening streets and after a quick supper fell gratefully asleep.

The first week was filled by the same routine. As Flora gained experience of the different kinds of job, from alterations to reworkings and complete new garments, she began also to understand the unspoken system by which the work was ordered and processed. Immediately above the table were the jobs in hand along with any urgent work that was to be given priority. This could only happen if instructed by Madame Guyon. The long wall behind was stocked several layers deep with the standard queue of garments which edged their way toward the upper end and finally the table. The business prospered.

Flora also became aware that the front counter and the workshop did not comprise the full extent of Madame Guyon's premises. A curtain to one side of the shop opened to reveal a steep stair and every so often Adrienne or Jeanne would be summoned to take a finished job up to a fitting room above. Then Madame would usher a customer up the stair. There were apparently four little rooms for fittings, and above that Madame Guyon's own apartment. Flora was kept to the back and did not meet any of the clients, though she could hear the voices in the front shop. At other times one of the women would be sent out to deliver a job for fitting elsewhere.

After, three weeks of working six days each week, Madame Guyon spoke to Flora in the front shop before she left.

'Your work is very satisfactory, Miss Flora. Is it not time now to leave the Convent and receive your own wages?'

'I have nowhere else to go, Madame Guyon.'

'I thought so. Bring your things here. There is a closet in the shop where you can sleep, behind the stair, and there is water at the pump in the back court. Then you can decide what to do. Do you want that?'

'Yes,' Flora heard herself saying.

'Good, then I will speak to Sister Teresa.'

So that was settled. Flora's apprenticeship was over. A week later on the Monday she left her refuge with a bundle of possessions and Sister Teresa's tearful blessing.

From the moment Flora left the convent to stay in Madame Guyon's closet, she entered a different world. Until then she had been treated in Jean St Denis as an exotic who might at any time revert to the protection of religion. She had been handled with kid gloves. Now she was an equal in the ups and downs of ordinary city life. Immediately Jeanne and Adrienne became more expansive about the eccentricities of Madame Guyon and the foibles of her customers.

The accommodation was no more austere than St Teresa had provided. Flora had a small pallet which she could roll up by day. It was warm in the closet and after she got beneath the blanket she could leave the curtain partly open for light and air. It was like a child's bedroom and she relished her lonely and silent possession of the shop during the hours of curfew. After closing hours Flora also had the run of the little back court with its pump and stone drain. There were stone shelves at the back door where she could keep bread, cheese and fruit from the street stalls. Madame Guyon's wages allowed the seam-stress to add small coin to the little bag of money she had carried from Boulogne.

During working hours Flora was now sent out and about like the others to fit clothes and deliver finished jobs. She quickly became familiar with St Honoré, and the surrounding street as far as the Tuileries in one direction, and the Seine bridges in the other. She was startled to find that the Palais Royal was just round the corner from Jean St Denis. This was where Charles Edward had been abducted by the French authorities, after refusing to leave Paris. He had been seized in the colonnade after attending the opera, thrown into a coach, and unceremoniously bundled out of the country.

Not only had the French made peace with Britain but Charles was uncomfortably popular, the young hero who had personally led his people into battle against the Hanoverians. Flora went cautiously through the archway by the theatre to see the gardens and courts beyond. It was a different ordered world, just yards from the noisy chaos of the main thoroughfare. Ideal for kidnapping.

Flora was nervous, intruding on the past, in case it tried to claim her. That episode had been the start of Charles' incognito, living in disguise like a spy or fugitive. At the work table Jeanne and Adrienne were full of gossip about the Young Prince still being hidden in the city. Glengarry had disdained disguise. playing only himself. But that had been his most deceitful part.

Later in the shop Flora mentioned her brief visit to the Palais Royal, and asked about if opera was still performed there. The others looked at her in surprise and burst out laughing.

'You haven't noticed,' spluttered Adrienne.

'What?' asked Flora, 'noticed what?'

'All these costumes,' gestured Jeanne, 'nobody wears that old stuff now.'

'They're for singers and actors, Flora, you Convent goose. Madame Guyon's famous for her theatre fittings.'

Flora blushed to the roots of her dark hair. Of course her ideas of court fashion were years out of date. She just did not notice that many of the outfits were out of date too. Presumably Madame Guyon had not mentioned this side of her business to Sister Teresa, as theatres and convents did not mix well. Then Flora started to laugh too.

'What a fool. I am not safe to be let out of a convent.'

'You're not and that's the truth,' scolded Jeanne, 'someone might take advantage.' This set both of them off again, and Flora found herself laughing along in some kind of strange relief. Then Madame Guyon's tall shadow loomed over the threshold.

'Very amusing, ladies, I am most sure. But we are behind with these jobs.'

'Yes, Madame Guyon'

'Of course, Madam, just drawing breath.'

The three women glanced at each other as they picked up their seams, forcibly suppressing another outburst of merriment.

The next day, Madame Guyon sent Flora to an apartment in Richelieu Street up from the Palais Royal. A richly ornamented dress was to be fitted privately for a famous though rather elderly opera singer.

'You take this one, Flora, for it is mainly your work, and very fine work it is too. Marie Pélissier is a woman who understands quality, unlike some that might be mentioned. Tact is needed also, my dear, for Madame is not a young woman. You I believe have the tact, unlike some that might be mentioned.'

Flora hurried into the front shop to wrap the altered dress before either of the others might catch her eye, or Madame Guyon's imperious gaze. Soon she was out onto the street where a bright midday sun lent the usual cacophony an air of temporary cheer. Richelieu Street took her in a quieter direction where the crumbling wood and plaster facades of Jean St Denis gave way to the handsome stone facades of town houses interspersed with elegant apartments. She found the address and the concierge let her up.

'Knock loudly,' she warned, 'Madame Pélissier is getting deaf.'

Up meant four floors with stairs narrowing at each level. The last flight was steep, finishing at a substantial door. Flora knocked loudly. And again.

'Don't hammer, I'm coming.'

The door inched open and a grey cropped head peered round.

'Is that the dress?'

'Yes, Madame Pélissier, from Madame Guyon.'

'There's no need to Madame me or her for that matter. You'd better come in.'

The head turned and Flora followed obediently down a dim hall into a spacious room whose windows opened onto the rooftops of Paris.

'What's your name?

'Flora, Madame –'

'Call me, Francesca, I like to pretend I am Italian. All the best parts are Italian.'

'This is the altered dress. I hope Ma – you will approve.'

The woman before Flora was swathed in a gorgeously coloured silk robe. It seemed to be an Indian or some kind of Asiatic pattern. The narrow face above was high boned but drawn, an effect heightened by the cropped hair which Flora realised had been deliberately bleached of colour. Oblivious to Flora's scrutiny, Francesca was shaking out the dress, straightening the ribbons and flounces.

'Hold this,' she commanded, 'taking the costume by the shoulder. Then she unwrapped the robe and holding long thin bare arms forward she bent towards the skirts. Flora lifted from the foot and began to pull the lower layers over Francesca's head, while the actress tunnelled expertly towards the neckline. As the narrow head re-emerged, Flora went round in circles tugging the fabric down.

'Gently woman, I'm not a marionette.'

But as Flora stepped back the effect was striking. Madame Pélissier seemed to dominate the room. Her presence was physically enlarged but also more regal and remote. She herself edged gingerly forward and then back, side to side, examining the results in an ornately framed full length mirror. As images of the moving costume appeared from different directions, Flora realised that the room was full of mirrors set at different heights and angles.

'Very good, no, excellent, my dear. Could you please arrange the bustle?'

Flora smoothed the curving silks round the rear hoops and patted the ribbons into place. The colours were deep greens and purples that shimmered in the light.

'What neat, clever little finger you have, Flora. I am sure that this dress is your work. What a success I shall be.'

Francesca made bolder sweeps to right and left allowing

the weight of the skirts to swing behind her body.

'The movement is superb. You, my dear, are an artist. Now, off with it, and we shall take coffee.'

The duet now went in reverse until the dress was eased back over Madame Pélissier's head.

'Not on the ground, I insist,' chided Francesca, in her shift 'see, here.'

She pointed Flora to a full height wooden stand with extended arms where the whole assemblage could be hung, and watched closely as Flora shook out the dresses and pulled the garment out to its full dimensions. Francesca was humming with pleasure as she wrapped the robe back round her gaunt frame. She had shrunk back to normal dimension.

'Good. Now, you may pour the coffee.'

Flora dutifully poured from a metal pot into two china cups, which were already laid out on the marble surface of a high table. She brought one over and handed it to Francesca who had reclined onto a couch. Then she brought over the second cup and was waved into an adjacent chair.

'So, am I an awful fright?' Flora began to choke on her coffee. 'No need to answer, or lie. I know I am. But you see, my dear, it's not the body that counts but its effect. On the stage, at least. I shall be wigged, and painted with high shoes to push the dress up and outwards. It will be Magnifica. They will cheer me to the rafters.'

'I am pleased you like the dress. The fabrics are very fine.'

'Why will they cheer me to the rafters?'

'I don't know – though no doubt your performance will –'

'You don't know very much about the theatre, do you?'

'No, I don't, only some childhood memories from Rome.'

'How sweet. They will cheer, even if I sing badly, because it is my benefit, the retirement of Francesca Pélissier, once the darling of Maestro Rameau. Which is why, dear Flora, I am pleased that even if I sound dreadful I shall look magnificent. I want you to come to the opera and help me dress.'

'Me, to the opera?'

'Who else am I addressing? The clothes horse?'

'I'll ask Madame Guyon. I would like to come very –'

'Tell old starch face that I need you.'

'What opera will you play?'

'It's just scenes, with some music and dancing between. A confection between dinner and supper. But I shall reprise my role as Emilie. She is loved by the Grand Vizier Osman. He is a Turk of course but gracious and tender. Yet Emilie is naturally loved by another. It is a scenario of love with seduction and desire. It was my great success when younger.'

'I don't know that opera.'

'The Amorous Indies of Rameau, a very popular piece. But that is beside the point. How shall I play it in my mature years?'

Madame Pélissier, then Francesca, now Emilie, fixed her expressive dark eyes on Flora and waited.

'I suppose, Madame, might suggest with gestures,' and she moved her own hands tentatively, 'and of course with the beauty of her voice.'

'Well, the voice, let me tell you, my dear, is a fragile reed. These days I pipe to only a single tune but Emilie is exactly my range. Is that not remarkable? I can be a younger woman in effect – through my sound and my costume. I am reborn in their emotions. And perhaps in a few memories. Of the most respectable sort, naturally. It is the magic of art. Of course there is the ballet too, which provides young bodies for the vulgar taste.'

'It will be a triumph, I am sure,' affirmed Flora tuning in to her expected chord.

The pale, worn face broke into a lovely smile. 'You are the wise one, are you not, my dear. And very pretty with it, in a kind of saturnine manner. Well, enough time wasted. I have my perfumier and wig dresser coming, and you are wanted back at the dragon Guyon's. I expect you at the theatre for 3.oopm exactly. Just ask for me and don't be late.'

With that dismissal, Flora let herself out and hurried down the stairs, relieved but excited. Walking back to the shop, she rehearsed how best to relay Francesca's peremptory orders to her own Madame. But Madame Guyon was unexpectedly complacent.

'Of course, Miss Flora, you will go to the theatre and dress Pélissier. She is an old client and a very great artist. There you will learn another side of my business.'

Looking back, Flora wondered if her visit to Marie Pélissier had been another test. At the time she was too caught up in the immediate task to have second thoughts. Reporting to the side door at the theatre, she was sent along dark passages and up narrow steps till she found the cramped side gallery in which the singers were being dressed. Little of that business of tucking and pinning remained in Flora's mind; her hands worked deftly without supervision. It was waiting in the wings to propel the elegant clothes-horse of Francesca onto the stage that captured her senses. She had never seen a theatre from this side. Here was the machinery of scenic movement, the marshalling of dancers to match cues from the pit, effects of light or dark, and the visual play of costume against animating flesh. Extraordinarily, spectators mingled with mechanics in the wings enjoying the spectacles of illusion and artifice.

Flora felt that Francesca had given a good account of herself before a thin house. At any rate some venerable admirers waited for her with flowers and champagne wines, sweeping her away in full regalia to celebrate. But Pélissier was only the first of many singers, male and female, to whom Flora was assigned for personal attentions, both in their home and at the theatre as performances loomed. Leading performers were expected to provide and maintain their own costumes, so possessing the best wardrobe was a cause of rivalry and of artistic prowess.

Madame Guyon was very satisfied with her investment in Flora who combined superb needlework, with colour sense, and a sympathy for the artistic temperament which she herself found impossible to muster. A few months after Flora had started to concentrate on the theatre clients, Madame Guyon summoned her upstairs to the private apartment and poured tea.

'You are happy here, Miss Flora?'

'Yes, Madame, I enjoy the work.'

'You take pleasure mostly in the theatre work.'

'Yes, I do, but I am willing to do all the jobs.'

'Thank God. These actors are sent by Him to try us. But never mind of that. I want you to be happy and stay here, not in another apartment.'

'Yes, Madame Guyon, I am very grateful for your accommodation though sometimes I am –'

'I want you to have my upper apartment to live in for yourself.' Flora looked round in puzzlement. 'Above, in the eaves. Would you like that?'

'Yes, I think so.'

'It will only mean a small deduction from the wages which I must increase soon for your skill, more than the others.'

Flora was shown up to the attic floor by way of a wooden ladder which stood just outside Madame's front door. Beneath the sloping roof there was a little window onto the sky, a tiny dresser, a rolled up mattress and a washstand. There was a small fireplace with brick chimney. It was a completely private space. She moved her bundle of surviving possessions up on the same day.

Flora had a profession and her own place to live; she thought less about the past and enjoyed accumulating some things to make the attic more comfortable. She bought a small mirror with a painted frame, a brush with a back made of shell, a kettle, some earthenware bowls and two china cups and saucers. It could be very hot in the eaves or very cold, but she was allowed a fire in winter, while in summer she bought food daily from the market and stored it on a stone shelf downstairs. Living simply she gradually accumulated a supply of money from Madame Guyon's wages supplemented by occasional tips from satisfied customers. It was some form of security.

Flora's reputation spread in the tightly knit gossipy world of theatre. Most of Madame Guyon's business was with the opera performers at the Palais Royal round the corner from Jean St Denis. But there was also the French theatre company on the other bank of the Seine, and various Italian troupes operating in the city. Though all of these companies carried a stock of costumes for minor roles and choruses, the main players were expected to supply their own. Competition was keen and Flora was kept constantly busy with making and altering for stage display the kind of garments which her royal mistress had once worn as a daily routine.

Her favourite moments were in the Opera House when, after applying some final costume adjustments, she could watch a performance from the side of the stage. What fascinated her was the accumulation of skills required to sustain the appearance of the action – carpenters, painters, costumiers, musicians, librettists and of course the composer. Having only experienced things from the auditorium, Flora could not understand why spectators were permitted to mill about on stage between scenes and watch from the wings. It seemed to destroy the artistic illusion. More so, since a kind of chaos prevailed back stage. There was a supervisor supposedly directing proceedings, but the scenic designer might also be there insisting on some changed angle, while individual performers manoeuvred to secure the best positions. Timings suffered in consequence but audiences seemed inured to gaps in the action, gossiping and commenting loudly on the performers and sets. They considered themselves to be the main performance; the stage action was an entertaining distraction.

Flora also gleaned from the never ending complaints of her customers that the overall organisation of the opera was equally chaotic. Everything ran on debt so that constant pressure was required for anyone to secure payment. The leading singers were in a strong position in this game of beggar-my-neighbour. They demanded their fees before consenting to a run of successful performances, while also receiving gratuities from admirers of both sexes. Dancers by contrast were often left in direst need since replacements could usually be found. Fortunately Madame Guyon's trade was with the lead performers, and she extracted payment mercilessly before delivering work for fitting and final adjustments. Hence her nickname, 'the Dragon'.

Flora dressed herself plainly but neatly in garments of her own making to avoid notice. Her only indulgence was a light tartan shawl that she found in a street market and wore pinned round her shoulders in all outside weathers. Accepted as a familiar presence she was able to move freely around the Palais. Because she sought no attention for herself, she became the recipient of many grumbles, confidences and gossip. Listeners in the world of theatre were a much scarcer commodity than talkers. In that way it was very like court life, but here there was an easy familiarity between the sexes. Also, unlike the audience which was wealthy and aristocratic, the back stage community included people of all classes and many nationalities. Speaking Italian and English, as well as French and a smattering of Spanish, Flora felt at home in this cosmopolitan world. Only her childhood Gaelic again lay fallow.

Flora would rise early, boil a kettle on her little hob, and enjoy coffee and a roll in her attic refuge. Then it was down to the work room where she was already through her first jobs when Jeanne and Adrienne arrived, and the morning banter began. The two other women accepted Flora without resentment because they recognised her skills as a dressmaker. But they were also avid for theatre gossip, and teased Flora mercilessly about 'relations with the actors', and 'the temptations of that wicked place'.

After an early lunch of bread and cheese, Flora would set out on her theatre rounds. With Madame Guyon's approval this now involved visiting the theatre and adjacent apartments to solicit work, as well as delivering completed costumes for fitting. If she could manage it, Flora liked to watch the beginning of the late afternoon performance before returning to the shop to work on into the evening.

One afternoon, coming through the auditorium, Michel Arres, the librettist, whom she knew by name, stopped to speak to her, perhaps for lack of someone more important to harangue.

'Would you believe it! That old fart Fuselier is agitating

in his rag for a revival. Journal of the arts classical, he calls it. A bundle of tittle-tattle completely out of date and bereft of artistic distinction, of art in fact.'

'What revival?'

Arres was a tall grandiloquent youth with long fair hair, all his own, which he swept back periodically. His overweening confidence had, to Flora's eye, an uncomfortable air of Glengarry. He claimed to be a Lorrainer but sounded Flemish.

'Amorous Indies of course. Do you not know it? He wrote the original libretto and wants it revived.'

'I thought it was always being revived. I made some costumes –'

'Only in scenes,' corrected Arres impatiently. 'It's not been done as a whole opera for years, decades even. And no wonder. The plot's all over the place. There isn't a plot, just disconnected stories. Rameau could never bear a plot obscuring his music. "You're going too fast" the singers would say, "No-one can make out the words". "Excellent," pronounces the Master, "Faster!"'

'Can you not revise the text?' queried Flora.

'With Fuselier breathing over every line in his filthy Journal? It's insupportable. How can audiences used to Voltaire's plays bear such pap?'

'What is your opera's theme? I thought Monsieur Voltaire's plays were very controversial with the public.'

'Controversial, my dear woman, is what the public crave. These exotic gallants are old-fashioned lovers, served up as soufflé for starters and every course thereafter. The old fool exudes sentimental virtue in every pore, while over the river at the Comedy they gorge on illicit passions. How can I compete with that? My reputation is in tatters working in this house.'

'Surely some changes must be possible?', suggested

Flora wondering in which other house Arres had flourished or even featured.

'There, there, read it for yourself. I am expected at Cafe Procope.'

With that, Michel shook his mane once more and rushed off to hang out at the most fashionable artistic cafe in town. Flora was left holding a batch of ruffled papers. She had never seen a complete libretto before as the performers with whom she worked only had copies of their own parts, adorned with scribbled cues. Madame Pélissier had performed in the premiere of Amorous Indies and made its scenes her swan song. Flora wondered what had become of the veteran singer, whose custom at Madame Guyon's had dried up after her retirement. She tucked the script down the side of a roomy canvas bag which carried the costumes.

That evening Flora finished early in the workroom and, foregoing supper in favour of some scraps of dried meat and bread, she retreated to her eyrie to read. There were four acts but each told a different tale, as Arres had complained. Yet there was a connecting thread in which two men competed for the love of a woman. The exception was Act Three in which the love tangle involved two women and one man. In every Act however the difficulties were resolved through devices ranging from a volcanic eruption to union of the right lovers – or rejection of both suitors.

Flora could see that these happy resolutions could not please an appetite for social transgression and tragic denouements in the style of Voltaire. Yet could audiences not enjoy more than one kind of theatre? The main interest for Flora was the different settings of Fuselier's stories. The first act was Turkish, the second set in Peru amongst the Incas, the third in Persia, and the fourth in the Americas amongst native tribes. Here surely was the point of the piece, enabling Rameau to reflect encounters with these exotic cultures through his music, playing at once upon the ear and the feelings. But what of the eye? How could such variety be costumed or painted?

In an instant, Flora was in the hall of Castle McIvor, each Highlander festooned in the folds of his checked plaid, held with a deerhide belt from which jutted pistol butts or the carved bone of a dagger hilt. Eagle's feathers swept up from their bonnets. Hung on the walls were studded leather bound shields, and the basket guards of claymores. So each people showed their character in colour and pattern.

She pulled herself back to the opera.

It was true that the relationships as described in the libretto were touching rather than moving. Yet Madame Pélissier's last performance as Emilie in Act One, released by the Grand Vizier to be reunited with her true love Valère, had been effective. When the music, costume and movement were brought together deep emotion might be evoked. But were Voltaire's betrayals and tragedies not more true to life than Rameau's melodious couplings? The Amorous Indies depended for its success on everyone's innate capacity to feel and love – audience and performers. What if someone were born cold, calculating and heartless? With at the same time the ability to charm and convince.

Flora pushed the script to one side.

Why had she not seen through Glengarry's mask to the frozen emptiness beneath? She had been trapped by her own emotional need, locked in numb grief. Gradually the paralysis had passed away, but anger and shame at what had happened still churned inside her without release.

Eventually she got ready for bed, pushing hurtful feelings aside. Before settling to sleep, she slipped the libretto under her pillow, wishing for happier dreams.

A few days later Flora was again at the Palais which was alive with talk of the forthcoming revival. Amorous Indies was in its separate parts staple fare of the opera programme, so there was curiosity and scepticism about the original fabled work. Singers were already campaigning for leading roles, with which as Flora knew the libretto was amply provided.

The disjointed episodes that played now in the repertoire were elaborately cosseted with dance sequences. They used well worn costumes from standard stock and scenery painted to suit almost any performance. Curiosity drew Flora to the stage where she knew that Bouchier, the scene designer, often worked. Sometimes they would both be frantically finishing last minute jobs there as the performances got underway.

She found Bouchier slumped over two long trestle tables placed end to end on stage left. He was a slight figure often shabbily dressed and normally hard at work with a contained energy that could fire up if things were not going according to his ideas.

'Excuse me, but I was wondering about Amorous Indies. How –'

Bouchier raised a hand to halt Flora's enquiry and then gestured wearily to the table.

'Here, Miss Flora, are temples of the east, palaces of Constantinople, even the tépees of the American natives. As for the Incas I have found a picture of their dress but not their buildings which seem to have been vast edifices in the jungle. Maestro Rameau has ransacked the globe in search of his scenarios.'

Flora moved closer to the extended table and looked at the prints that Bouchier had laid out.

'These are magnificent.' she murmured, 'a new scene for each episode.'

'Indeed, so you might suppose. But how can we paint this worn out old lady of a house, never mind move four sets? Tell me that!'

'Surely the carpenters –'

'Look here,' insisted Bouchier, jumping to his feet and pulling Flora after him. 'See, every piece has to be dragged into position like some ancient siege machine. Where are the grooves to roll flats? Where are the winches for winding up multiple backcloths? Nowhere. Every modern theatre has them. The Comedy has them but here we live in medieval times. It is appalling. A scandal against art.'

'But, Maestro –'

'Please, just call me François.'

'If you please, but the opera is known for the finest scenic perspectives.'

'Yes, the work of Servandoni, a true Maestro whose shoes I am not fit to lace. That was ten years ago but we are still touching up his classical vistas. One for every performance, or if truth be told, one for several performances. We need something different.'

'Yes, Amorous Indies could be a scenic inspiration, Maestro, François.'

'Above all Amorous Indies. This is my chance, Flora, to finally design something fresh. But how? Even in Lisbon, where the city has been devastated by earthquake, they have built a theatre equipped with every modern contrivance. There you can be an artist. Here we are drudges, slaves to this cantankerous ruin of a Paris that once cherished our art.'

As his invective drained away, Bouchier's shoulders sank and he walked back to his seat. Flora followed him quietly back to the table.

'I have been reading the libretto.'

'Really. Thin stuff.'

'Yes, Arres lent me a copy. Perhaps there is another way to work. If one set could be designed to represent a foreign temple or palace, different trees could be added in front for each scene – palms or forest plants.'

There was a pondering silence.

'That is a possible idea.'

'Then also we could design different costumes for each scene, representing the different peoples.'

'But the costumes are all stock. Would singers buy new costumes?'

'I don't know. Only if I could adapt existing ones, or add something. Look at these feathers in the Inca dress.'

'Can you draw, Flora?'

'Once, I had lessons.'

'Then take these and sketch what you see.' Bouchier pushed a box of crayons towards her. 'Bring them in and we can touch up the colours against the scenery.'

Flora hesitated as if presented with some forbidden fruit. 'I am sorry but I have no paper.'

'Of course, take these sheets, and re-use the backs of these ones for roughs.'

Flora gathered everything into her canvas back where the libretto was nestling.

'You have not always lived in this way, have you, Flora? Was your family well born?'

'They were ruined by war.'

'Ah. I am sorry. I have noticed your costumes often. You have a gift. Bring me the sketches and let us see what can be done.'

'Yes, Maestro, thank you.' Flora left quickly before the gratitude she suddenly felt swelling up showed in her eyes. She hurried through the day's routine tasks so that she could make a start on this new venture. But even as her hands moved deftly, her mind was racing.

As it proved, the solutions were simple, even within the limited materials available. Over two evenings Flora thought and drew, working swiftly between paper and eye. She was not concerned with the polish or effect of her sketches, only with what they expressed in the shapes. For the male characters she concentrated on varying helmets and headdresses to suit. For the costumes she stripped back the normal attire of the classical hero to indicate native chiefs, complemented by feathers and ribbons. The Europeans retained classical garb, while the orientals were swathed in silk robes and turbanned. Even the house stock contained these items.

The female characters posed a harder challenge. Flora imagined various forms of half dress or undress, and laughed aloud at the hysteria that might cause. Even Voltaire would come running to the opera then. But Flora had an idea – if the leading ladies were persuadable. At least they already trusted her judgement.

For the foreign characters she would replace the traditional hooped skirts and bustle with swathes of silk and brocades, varied in colour and pattern to suggest a native identity. The underskirts and petticoats could be similarly diverse, though also increased in bulk so that the overall sweep and flow would have the same or even greater impact in movement than the conventional court dresses. This would involve expense yet if the singers felt the novelty might attract public attention... expectations of this production were mounting.

It was the last day of the week before Flora was able to look for Bouchier again at the theatre. The performances were over when she went back to the Palais in the evening. She liked that time when candles were burning low flickering in their brackets throwing a dim glow over the shabby back corridors. It was as is the whole creaking building was lit, ready to take the stage, even though the public had left. The auditorium itself was hushed and all that could be heard were the background noises of sweeping and tidying as the old labyrinth settled into its night of dreaming. Long forgotten artists waited in the shadows for their entrance.

Bouchier was in a green room where he had been chatting to performers as they left for home. Flora found him left behind with his thoughts, but she appeared to be a welcome interruption. Leafing through the drawings, Bouchier saw immediately what was intended.

'These are good. Small changes for the men, but will our divas go with these skirts? No-one has dressed like that before in opera.'

'I think so, the younger ones anyway. They want to make their mark.'

'And all the female roles are young. You are a clever woman, Flora, and beautiful with it.'

'Have you thought about the scene painting?'

'Yes, yes, I can do it, as you described. I'll colour up a sketch tomorrow now that I've seen these.' His mind seemed to be on other things. 'I have decided though to go to Lisbon after this production.'

'To the new theatre?'

'Yes, this place will never change. Will you come with me?'

Abruptly aware that Bouchier was standing close and willing her to meet his eyes, Flora could feel heat rising over her face.

'As an assistant?'

'If you wish.'

He put a hand on her arm but Flora stepped back a pace. 'You have children, a family.'

'What do you know of my family? Madame Bouchier will never leave France.'

'François, I am a... bereaved. I am bereaved and not able to... My past.'

'Come to Lisbon. I don't care about the past. There can be new worlds.'

'Wait.' She picked up the drawings. 'Wait.' She could not find an answer to him. 'You must take your family.'

'Think, dear Flora, think what life can still hold, before it is too late.'

She was in the corridor hurrying towards the stage doors. But suddenly a tall figure swayed into the dim light ahead.

'Who have we here? Ah, ah, little Flora! Excellent, come in and drink a toast.'

He manhandled her through an open door into a den of noisy merriment and shouting. 'Look,' cried Arres,' our lovely seamstress has come to join the party. We must drink to, to, to what?' He was pouring champagne unsteadily into half-full glasses. 'I know – To Amorous Indies! The worst script ever produced by Paris Opera.'

No-one paid the inebriated writer any attention as the company of seven or eight were sprawled around the room on chairs and sofas engaged in their own loud conversations or in one instance a drink fuelled embrace. Flora recognised several of the younger performers. One actress was still in a costume which Flora had recently let out.

Arres raised a full glass to his mouth forgetting to hand one to Flora. Then wiping his lips with one hand he pushed her towards the wall with the other, glass still in hand. She tried to slip down against the wall. Now he was fumbling with her tartan shawl. 'Let's show some bosom for the crowd,' he sneered.

Flora lashed out with her right foot and felt her wooden soled boot connect hard on the shins. But the broad bearded face above her looked more puzzled than pained, as if trying to locate the source of his annoyance. It was just enough for her to slip free, and though he lurched out in pursuit Flora was already round the corner and running for the door, clinging tightly to her canvas bag.

'Miss Flora, Miss Flora! Are you alright?'

It was old Pierre the doorman. She drew breath.

'Yes, thank you. The party is getting out of hand.'

'Don't tell me. That Flemish lout. He's not fit for decent company. You take your time now, Miss, he'll not get past me, if he's still on his feet.'

'I'll be home in a few minutes. Good night, Pierre.'

'Oh, Miss Flora. I nearly forgot. There's a message for you.'

He handed her a folded paper, but Flora did not wait to read it. She ran round the corner into Jean St Denis, and hurried upstairs to her attic, shutting the trap door firmly behind her. The last precaution was unnecessary as no unauthorised person would manage safe passage into Madame Guyon's lair.

Only then did she sit down panting and trembling by the empty hearth. Rather than think about what had just happened, Flora pulled out and unfolded her message. It was two lines long and read,

'Meet me tomorrow at noon in the Cour Royale. Do not tell or bring anyone else.'

It was signed 'Clementina Walkinshaw'.

Flora slept late after a troubled night. She knew it was Clementina's writing, yet she was reluctant and fearful.

The Cour was behind the theatre and its adjoining courtyard in the Palais Royal. It would be deserted at this time. How had Clementina known?

She waited before noon in the cover of the colonnade. She had put on a plain linen shawl with a bonnet and looked like any of the city's poor working women. As the bells of St Honoré and St Roche beyond struck twelve, a tall figure entered the court from the theatre side and slipped into the arcade. As Flora walked towards the other woman she knew it was Clementina Walkinshaw. As Clementina approached Flora saw she was dressed from head to foot in black velvet and that her face was completely covered by a black veil hanging from her broad brimmed hat.

'Are you alone?' Clementina's voice hissed from behind the veil in a stage whisper.

'Yes.'

'And you told no-one?'

'I know no-one here, Clementina. How did you find me?'

'Through the Sisters, but indirectly. I am being pursued.'

'By whom?'

'Charles. He is determined to recover my child, Louisa.'

'Is he here in Paris?'

'He is everywhere, Flora, a master of disguise and subterfuge. When I was with him we wandered all over but he has a secret refuge here in Paris. Many women shelter him even now.'

'This is where he was seized by the French, after the opera.'

'I know. So we should be safe here. What are you doing in such a place?"

'Why did you leave him, Clementina, taking the child?'

'Charles is a ruined man. A slave to vice. Drinking, gambling and worse. I feared for my life, and for the child.'

'What will you do?'

'Flora, you must not tell.'

'I have no-one to tell, believe me.'

'We are in the care of good Sisters, and in communication with the Court in Rome.'

'Palazzo Muti!'

'Hush, Flora!' Clementina glanced round anxiously but the Cour was abandoned. 'I am asking for the king's protection, and that of the Cardinal Henry. I have already shown my loyalty to them, so that my child will be properly brought up as a princess of the blood.'

'And when Charles succeeds?'

'Then he will have to recognise her.'

This was a glint of the old commanding Clementina, though with hardened metal.

'What do you need from me?'

'Nothing. I wanted to see you before… well before. I have no illusions left, Flora, whatever you might think. I will be shut up somewhere till Louisa is grown and then I will be permanently enclosed, out of sight. I am the scarlet woman.'

Flora wanted to offer some qualifying comfort but was unable to deny the truth of what Clementina had said.

'Why are you here, Flora?' Her friend filled the gap.

'Surviving, working to live, as a seamstress and costume maker for the opera.'

'How dreadful. You were always clever with your hands.'

Flora could not help smiling at this flash of the old Clementina.

'Come somewhere to eat with me, Clementina, and we can have a proper talk.'

'I daren't. I see spies everywhere. But we can walk for a minute here. It's very quiet.'

So the two friends, one tall and richly garbed, the other below medium height and plainly clothed, walked arm in arm in the sheltered gallery. And Flora listened to an account of Clementina's wanderings with Charles, to news of Rose's children and happiness with Waverley, of O'Sullivan's retirement to Italy, and even of Glengarry. He had returned to Scotland and succeeded his father as chief. Though suspicions were rife, he had not been declared a traitor. His double game continued.

'You were well rid of that viper, Flora,' pronounced Clementina.

'He betrayed us all.'

'I am sure that King James will take you under his protection in Rome. I sent them an account of your troubles and Glengarry's double dealing.'

'I am not sure that I want to go back to the Palazzo.'

'You can't go on living like this. I suppose you're safe here though.'

'As long as no-one knows.'

'I must go, Flora, or I will be missed. When I get to Rome I will send you a message. Then you can decide what to do.'

'Thank you, Clementina, and thank you for coming to look for me.'

'We must not lose touch, dear Flora.'

'Let me see your face. Please. Clementina.'

The tall figure hesitated and then lifted her veil. There was the upturned nose and the high cheekbones but the skin was discoloured. It was the face of a woman who had suffered blows. Flora kissed her tenderly on both cheeks and raising her arms lowered the veil. For one moment they were lost in each other's embrace. Then Clementina tore herself away and hurried out of the Cour.

Flora sat down alone on the stone edge of the colonnade

and cried without restraint. She had not wept like this since Boulogne.

The next two weeks were a blur of frantic activity. The opening of Amorous Indies had been brought forward due to the failure of the current production after only four performances. Flora rushed from the shop to singers' apartments to the theatre and back to Madame Guyon's. Her fingers never stopped, while her mind was gratefully numb.

The unexpected panic also worked in favour of the new designs as everyone was caught up in the need to get a performance ready for the public. Singers agreed to the costume changes and urged Flora to bring their fittings forward. It was one of those rare times when all parts of the huge unwieldy mechanism that was the opera seemed to move in the same direction.

At the Palais carpenters and scene painters were also busy. Bouchier supervised the work with intense energy, barely acknowledging interruptions. Flora kept out of the designer's way until the rehearsals when all the elements were brought together. As usual at this juncture chaos prevailed while the Director struggled in vain to marshal his resources in the right order. However cries and gasps of astonishment greeted the finished scene cloths, while both singers and dancers flaunted their new costumes. No-one could recall a production that had been so completely renewed. Excitement mounted; there was a whiff of success in the aether.

On the first night Flora was furiously busy with final adjustments. She ran from each dressing room to the wings where dancers were gathering. Everything had to be finished at the same time. She was oblivious to the rapidly filling auditorium, or the coaches queuing in Rue

St Honoré to offload the cream of fashionable society. As boxes became crammed and the stalls filled spectators crowded into the corridors or onto the stage, delaying the opening curtain.

But nothing now could halt the momentum. The director gave a signal for the music to begin. Cheers greeted the scenery, especially the change of trees with each Act. Whenever a character appeared for the first time they too were cheered. The female costumes were a sensation. The dancers, normally ignored, were accorded a standing ovation in their own right. The singers excelled amidst the adulation, while Rameau's old magic wove its spell. Lovers were parted and united, suitors rejected, and true devotion rewarded.

The house dissolved in wild applause. Encores were called and given. Backstage people embraced without restraint. It was a triumph. Amidst the confusion, François seized Flora by the shoulders, and looking into her eyes kissed her lips. Then he released her and merged back into the melée. When Flora eventually crept away from the Palais, after hanging up as many costumes and salvaging as many feathers as she could, the party was in full swing.

Success followed night after night in a crescendo not experienced by the house for years, or so the journals claimed. Fuselier, the venerable librettist, was exultant in the press and also attended nightly to witness the applause. Michel Arres had not been seen in the Palais since the night of his drunken assault, absenting himself from a triumph in which he had no part. Flora became very tired and struggled to keep up with routine work at the shop, though Madame Guyon was understanding, and appreciative of the money which Amorous Indies earned, as the numerous costumes continued to need repair and adjustment.

After another busy night at the theatre, Flora came downstairs one morning later than normal. Sister Teresa was sitting in a chair in the shop while Madame Guyon was at her station behind the counter. The extra chair had been brought out especially for the Sister, who looked in this strange setting like the old lady she was. Teresa rose as Flora appeared and smiled quietly towards her, slightly inclining her head.

'I have a message for you, Flora, from Mother Abbess.'

She was unable to move or speak. Madame Guyon stared at her alarmed at what this intrusion from the Convent might mean. Teresa sensed the strain and stepping forward touched Flora's arm.

'It is nothing to fear. I think a letter has come for you,' she said quietly

The Sister did not understand that this news was not as reassuring as intended. Flora pulled on her plain shawl, and the two women left Rue St Denis for the Convent. There Flora was taken directly to the Abbess without greetings or small talk.

Mother Abbess was formal and businesslike as if she belonged to another alien world. She did not ask how Flora was getting on, as if it was none of her concern or she already knew and did not approve.

'I have received this package for you, Flora. It has come from Rome. You will understand from whom it has come. It has come with strict instructions that I am to give it to you in person and see you open it in my presence.'

She handed over a small bundle of tightly folded papers which were bound with an elaborate seal. Then she passed over a paper knife and Flora duly broke open the waxen arms of the Royal House of Stuart.

The first page was a formal letter addressed to her as the Honourable Miss Flora McIvor of the House of

McIvor. It proceeded in courtly fashion, but the intent was that His Majesty King James was graciously pleased in recognition of the loyal service of those bearing the name of McIvor to grant the said Miss McIvor, in renewal of the gift of Her Late Majesty Clementina Sobieski, an annual pension of sixty Louis d'Or. Beneath this letter was a bank draft in her name drawn against a banking house in Paris. This was carefully signed and sealed at the foot with a smaller version of the same royal emblem.

'Is it all complete, and clear?'

'Yes, I think so,' replied Flora barely registering the crisp tone.

'Could you please sign this to confirm you have received the papers?'

Flora took the proffered pen and signed the additional paper which the Abbess had prepared.

'Well, Flora, I do not pretend to understand your affairs, or your reasons, but this may be an opportunity to make amendment in your life.'

'Yes, Mother Abbess.'

'God go with you, my child.'

The interview had been concluded. Flora was ushered out of the study clutching her papers. There was no sign of Teresa, and she was shown through the double barred doors by a silent nun into the blinking light of early morning Paris.

Ignoring the curious glances, Flora climbed back into her loft. First she smoothed out the papers and read through both the documents again. There was no doubt as to their authenticity. Next she pulled out her surviving possessions from under the truckle bed. She unwrapped and laid out the miniature portraits of her father and mother, the lock of Fergus' hair when still a boy, the garnet brooch mounted in tarnished silver which she had been given at Castle McIvor, her prayer book, some pieces of antique lace, her last formal dress, and the sketches she had made for the opera. She watched for a lingering while and then left everything open to view, going back to her tasks in the workroom.

That afternoon she went earlier than usual to the Palais in order to seek out François. He seemed surprised to meet her in his realm.

'You are early today, Flora. I did not expect to see you before the performance.'

She looked rather than spoke her question.

'Of course, you realise I cannot go to Lisbon. That is out of the question now after my, our, success. There is talk of a new theatre here in Paris, built for the opera.'

'Yes, I understand. Will you write a letter of recommendation for me to the Lisbon Opera?'

'You want to leave Paris after such acclaim?'

'Will you write the letter?'

'My feelings for you, Flora, are not tied to Lisbon. Don't take this change in the wrong way.'

'But you will write.'

'If you insist, yes.'

'Thank you, François. I will collect it before the end of the week.'

'Don't trouble yourself. I'll leave it with Pierre at the stage door.'

Flora nodded and left, relieved to accept her dismissal without an extended scene. She had no more emotion to commit. In a fortnight at the most Amorous Indies would have run its gilded course and she would be free to go without obligation or regret.

5

EARLY EVENING WAS Flora's favourite part of the day. The sun had declined from its fierce afternoon heat. There was an audible breathing out from workaday routine as people took the cooler air, wandering up the hill to enjoy the sinking western light and breezes from the estuary. Lisbon lived by the cycle of the sun. Even in wetter seasons the rain blew over and some warmth was restored in these evening hours.

'Miradouro' they called it, and builders were now constructing a great sunlit terrace beside the Church of Santa Luzia. Locals quietly ignored architectural hyperbole, and continued to enjoy the rays of a setting sun as their diurnal right and habit. Miradouro was a golden ripple in a tongue that everyone in this city could speak, even in the Alfama, its poorest district.

It was hard to believe that she had been here for more than two years. Such was the pace of life and the regularity of her existence. Each day Flora rose early to walk down the hill, through the valley where the builders were still hard at work on Lisbon's new clean cut streets and squares, amidst a tangle of scaffolding, ropes and rubble. This was where the tidal wave had swept in after the earthquake taking thousands of lives. Then she climbed up an even steeper slope on the other side to where the handsome Teatro de São Carlos stood catching its first gleams of sunlight.

She worked all day there in the rooms set aside for making and storing costumes. Most people went home for siesta before the late afternoon performance but Flora stayed on, leaving as the performance began. She would then retrace her steps in the early evening as the heat of the day receded.

It seemed that this pattern had been prepared awaiting her arrival. Yet when she fled Paris, and Flora recognised it now as flight, she had no idea what to expect. Bouchier had written her the promised letter of recommendation without further complaint, but Madam Guyon turned her back in speechless fury when she heard of Flora's decision to leave. Only the other women wept – sturdy Jeanne and Adrienne with her thin faded face – embraced their friend and wished her well.

The coach to Bordeaux and the sea voyage had been without incident, though a pleasant relief of airy sky and space after the closeness of Paris. She had become accustomed to that city's dirt and dark, taking her comfort from the dim illumination of the workroom, her attic, and the half-lights of the theatre world. Now Flora lived as much as she could by the open light of day.

The theatre was much more spacious and ordered here in the capital of Portugal. Rebuilt soon after the terrible earthquake São Carlos had every facility needed for modern design, designated spaces for the performers, and a permanent stock of well maintained costumes. That had been a welcome surprise, providing the newly arrived Flora with immediate employment. Left behind was the constant calling at apartments to tout for business. She was not earning as much as Madame Guyon had latterly paid, but life was cheaper in Lisbon and she had the precious pension unspent, carefully concealed at her lodgings. The work was undemanding, and suited the calmer tempo of Flora's existence. She felt safe, often drowsy in the warmth, and at peace.

The walk back down from the Miradouro was a gentle stroll in the shade. Below the ancient Cathedral, which had been damaged by the quake and still awaited repair, the narrow streets were coming into their evening life. The first candles were being lit and cooking smells rose from the side alleys and twisting lanes which led down through the warren towards the river. Small shops had reopened and stalls were uncovered selling food for the social hours ahead. Flora often shopped at these same stalls in the early morning or went down to the shore where the latest catch had been brought in by the fishermen. She only went to the city markets when buying fabrics for work.

Within five minutes Flora reached the junction of São Pedro and Rua Remedos where she turned into the familiar gateway of Villa Flor. The children came running to welcome Miss Flora, the Flora of Flor, and soon she was setting aside her basket and cotton shawl to head for the communal kitchen.

The Villa was a substantial house rising over the steeply sloping streets. The main rooms looked out onto the broad estuary which seemed more like an inland sea. Once it had been the residence of a rich merchant or nobleman, but such wealth had left Alfama long since, and now the main house was divided into apartments. A covered walkway led from the house above the street to a cobbled courtyard in which Flora lodged. This had been the servants' quarters which accommodated a wide range of families and itinerant workers in little rooms round three sides of the square. On the fourth side was the kitchen, washrooms and the home of Mãe Renata. In the centre of the courtyard was a well, sheltered by two gnarled trees beneath which were stone benches. Washing lines stretched in every direction from the trees to the pillars of a bleached wooden arcade that ran round the yard giving welcome shade to the doors and windows of the houses.

At this refreshing time of the day everyone was out in the courtyard. The men sat around smoking, cleaning and mending tools. Children ran about shouting and laughing, while the women clustered round the open fires of the kitchen gossiping and preparing evening meals. Most people ate communally at a long table in the yard, presided over by the mistress of Villa Flor.

No-one knew exactly the status of Mãe Renata or how the rule she exercised over her little kingdom had begun. However she let out the rooms, supervised the cleaning and cooking for tenants of the apartments over the walkway, and generally tended her brood like a dominating mother hen. Renata was plump, muscled and short, with abundant dark hair piled above her brow. She smelt of all the herbs that grew from old earthenware pots around the well, and nothing escaped her diligent care or remorseless right to know. When Renata moved about the Villa her whole person seemed to propel itself in a single motion without separate action of arms and legs.

As Flora joined the kitchen conference bringing her own small share of ingredients, the nightly drama was already getting underway. Ligia was preening herself for the expected visit of Jaiminho the stone cutter. Ligia was a bronzed, fair haired beauty whose striking looks made her a centre of attention. She served as Renata's assistant and maid of all work, but this did not preclude her dressing come the evening in flounced skirts, and a richly embroidered cotton blouse that showed off the upper body of a Juno to best effect. Flora had put her own hand to finishing that embroidery with an array of ribbons that owed something to the theatre wardrobe.

Jaiminho worked in the old Roman theatre above the Cathedral where stone was quarried and cut. He matched Ligia in stature, rich skin hues, and nobility of feature. The suitor would appear nightly as dinner drew to a close, scrubbed and shiny, and dressed in a plain white shirt open at the neck. Jaiminho was a forthright peasant turned urban worker. Like most of the Alfama's occupants he was drawn to the bustling, rebuilding capital by the lure of work paid in cash, but his dream was to return to the village and the life that was home. Ligia however had imbibed superior notions of herself from Mãe Renata and Villa Flor's tenuous contacts with respectability. She had become a city girl in aspiration at least, and looked down on Jaiminho at the same time as she sampled the fruits of his devotion.

Fun commenced while the noisy communal dinner was ending. Darkness had descended swiftly on the courtyard but lanterns and candles appeared on all sides, as the children were put to bed. Ligia flitted between kitchen, table and the well, which was lit by two or three lamps hung from the trees. Jaiminho pursued doggedly trying to draw his quarry into the dimmer recesses of the arcade, which was in turn draped with climbing plants that lent an enticing late summer aroma to the atmosphere.

Unfortunately for the expectant lover, the game was for someone to suddenly appear in the chosen recess with an errand for Ligia or just a friendly desire to chat. The quarry played her teasing role to the hilt, though being careful at some point to give a degree of tangible encouragement to the stonecutter. However, if as the evening revels came to their end, there was any hint of a more lingering dalliance, Renata whose eagle eye had registered every move in proceedings so far, would dash in chasing off Jaiminho into outer darkness.

Flora took no part in these games though she laughed with the rest. After dinner was cleared she went to her room to enjoy the last hour of the day in her own company. As the sociable chatter lessened a comfortable peace breathed through Villa Flor, leaving her alone yet not solitary. She unwound and rebraided her still dark hair, and kept her own small stock of garments in neat and attractive order, just like her chamber with its painted dresser, table and bed. Finally she drew a cloth over the open window to keep insects at bay, extinguished the lamp and lay down to rest. Sometimes memories crept in to delay sleep, but there were compensations to leaving youth behind. Most nights she slipped calmly into unconscious rest.

The two longer lasting occupants of Villa Flor's once grand main floors were a priest and a poet. Father José was, or had been, chaplain to a confraternity associated with the Cathedral though his current status seemed, like most of the Villa's tenants, indeterminate. He was however the firmly established favourite of Mãe Renata. She felt that the presence of a priest conferred prestige and dignity on her establishment, and in return she lavished special attentions on the complacent cleric, feeding and pampering his lean frame. Some unkind gossip suggested that she would not permit Father José to lie in an unwarmed bed.

The priest for his part went about his own business, whatever that might be, and exchanged greetings with the Villa's other inhabitants in passing. When he realised that Flora had Italian, he paused sometimes to share his memories of Rome. Renata hovered around these occasional conversations, buzzing approval like a queen Bee. She regarded Flora as a respectable woman down on her luck, and seemed to believe that she and the grey haired Father had much in common.

The other distinguished resident was known in Villa Flor as the Poet. His name was Lorenzo Gozzi, and like many of the cultured set in Lisbon he was Italian. Unlike the slightly shabby priest, the Poet dressed in some style and wore a carefully tended wig. He was compactly built of medium height, and carried himself with confident poise. He was considered eminent by Mãe Renata, and therefore by the whole community of Villa Flor which he generally ignored, so confirming their high opinion. Speculation regarding his marital status, requirements for a mistress and age were rife. He could certainly be described as handsome though in a mature kind of way. Renata had conceived a plan to marry the Poet to Ligia, so in one move raising up her protégé and retaining a valued tenant. Hence her virulent disapproval of the poor stonecutter.

One morning as Flora came into the courtyard after an early visit to the harbour stalls, she overheard an irate Renata fulminating in the washhouse. Some of the Alfama idioms were beyond her basic Portuguese but the meaning was plain.

'Where were you so late, slut? Do you think I am deaf or blind? If it were not waking a respectable house I would have got up to beat you then and there. You daughter of an ill-gotten bastard, are you trying to turn my good house into a brothel. After everything I have done for you. I had to take the Poet his eggs and fish in my own hands.'

The tone was sliding from anger towards hurt reproach.

'Nothing happened, Mãe. What's got into you today? I only went up the hill to make sure that oaf did not get drunk and end up in prison.'

'Look at your eyes, daughter, the lids can barely open. Is that how you will attract a gentleman?'

'Not this again, I don't want to marry any gentleman.'

'Be quiet, you disobedient hussy. You'll marry if I say so.'

'Not that old Poet, Mãe. That's just like being in service.'

'I'm not listening to another word from those shameful lips. You're burning for that uncouth Jaimhino, Ligia, I can see it. What can he bring in life except grief and labour? A peasant come to town. The head is as bare as his purse. Go and clean the rooms. And don't show your face in here again till they're spotless, and scrub your own skin clean while you're about it. Hussy.'

The last word was like a weary exhalation of breath as the culprit departed. Flora hurried on before a recalcitrant Ligia appeared in the doorway. The row would be made up before evening, but then the cycle would begin all over again.

It amused her to think of the Poet being subjected to Renata's marital scheming, like a victim of the comic opera plots that dominated the Lisbon stage. For in reality Lorenzo Gozzi wrote or at least adapted these plots for Teatro São Carlos. Flora had often seen the Poet holding court in the theatre foyer where he sold his libretti before performances. She had never spoken to him, nor had he deigned to notice the humble seamstress. After realising the librettist was also a tenant of Villa Flor, she had paid Gozzi little attention. What else did the Poet do, or was the opera his mainstay?

It came as a surprise when later that same week Lorenzo Gozzi spoke to her in the theatre. Flora was passing through the foyer in search of a singer who had missed his fitting. Gozzi was coming through the door directly in her path and stopped.

'You are the costume maker.'

'Yes, I work here.'

'Your work is very fine. All the artists wish to have your costumes.'

'Well not Luis Ferraro. He has not come to be fitted though he is due to sing as leading man tomorrow, and I must finish his costume.'

'Ferraro is a young fool, a libertine. He will be in his cups somewhere.'

'That is not my business, or concern, Maestro.'

'Maestro? You are mocking me, dear lady. The only thing I master here is hackwork.' Gozzi waved his new libretto in the air dismissively. 'You are more of a creator than I. But since we are both inmates of Villa Flor, we must drink wine or coffee together one afternoon. Here in the Chiado though, not in Alfama where the attentions of the fair Ligia may be loosed upon me at any moment.'

Flora could not help smiling at this tone, and for a second she met Gozzi's look. His eyes were light blue, almost grey, mobile with amused intelligence. He had noticed her. She quickly looked away but did not want to deny their moment of recognition.

'Mãe Renata is the stage director at Villa Flor. Now I must find Luis.'

'What about our coffee?'

'I don't frequent the coffee houses.'

'But you will be my guest.'

'Another time, perhaps, when this performance has opened.'

'Good day to you.' This to Flora's rapidly retreating back.

The first real conversation began on the following Monday, when La Serva Padrona was successfully launched.

There was no performance in the theatre so the singers and musicians stayed away and everyone else came in late. Flora liked these times when the big clear spaces of the new building were quiet and she could catch up on routine jobs undisturbed. But Gozzi appeared in the afternoon and invited her to join him for a drink. It transpired that he was well known in the cafe on the other side of the piazza from the theatre, where he conducted his business and socialised with the artists.

Flora had never crossed the threshold of Cafe São Carlos but when she arrived the librettist came out to make her welcome. They sat at an outside table in the sun where she soon relaxed, and enjoyed the unusual luxury of drinking coffee that had been prepared by someone else. Gozzi looked around him very much at his ease.

'Did you see the performance?'

'Most of it, though Serpina's aprons kept snagging. Whoever saw a serving woman with lace aprons?'

'Ah, but the lovely Nelidova is the beauty of the piece and must be flaunted. What about the plot?'

'I don't take much notice of the plots.'

'Because they are all the same.'

'Well, often.'

'Have you not heard Serva Padrona before?'

'Yes, in Paris where it caused a great row. There was a –'

'War of the operas, between followers of the French style and the comic Italians. You were there?'

'In a way. Costume makers don't take sides. I had to sew for both schools.'

'So was this production of the Padrona different?'

'Longer?'

'Indeed, dear lady, longer. Can I call you by your name? Flora. Twice as long, padded out from the two short acts of Pergolesi to four so that the good merchants of Lisbon can have their full evening of entertainment, and eat and drink and ogle to their lazy hearts' content.'

'How did you stretch it out?' asked Flora, remembering the loose plotting of Amorous Indies. 'Is the humour not in the action?'

'So you do follow the plots. Exactly, how to pad out without padding. Surely you face that problem in your craft as well. But for me it was easy. I looked at life.'

Gozzi paused to lean back in his chair as Flora laughed. He accepted her enjoyment appreciatively.

'Umberto the bachelor,' he continued, 'has a maidservant who thinks she is mistress of the household. Here is an extra act in the making. I introduce another character, the girl's mother, who is determined her wayward girl will marry this wealthy old Umberto. Do you recognise this story?'

'Just a bit.'

'The orchestra must roll out a few standard songs and we have the first Act. As for the rest we just enlarge the original. Of course at the end the mother too must join the household. Only the music – and Pergolesi is here a master – can convince us that this conclusion is happy. Surely in life Umberto and the Mãe would settle for each other?'

'And what of Serpina? Should she not have wed her soldier instead of the crusty old bachelor?'

'The soldier is merely a decoy, Serpina's tool in disguise. But suitors are queuing at the door. If only she chooses wisely.'

'Do you believe in happy endings?'

'The Italians insist on them, and so now do the Portuguese.'

'We cannot play Orpheus and lose Eurydice.'

'Not here. How did you come to costume making, Flora?'

She was disconcerted by this sudden directness, but she had a stock reply in hand.

'I lost my nearest family in war. They joined the struggle to restore the House of Stuart in Britain. We were, are, Scottish, from the Highlands of that country, but exiled. It is far away now, a long story. I have left it behind and take no part in politics.'

'Perhaps one day you will tell me that story.'

The conversation moved on to other lighter topics, until it was time for Flora to go back and tidy up her day's work.

The next week they met again, until gradually it became two or three times a week, depending on the theatre schedule. But by unspoken agreement they continued to ignore each other at Villa Flor. This was a friendship formed by shared interests and the pleasure each took in the other's company. It was their own to enjoy, without interference. Flora had never experienced such friendship with a man, though she sensed that Lorenzo had known women of all kinds.

Bit by bit she pieced together a picture of Gozzi's life. He had been born in a poor family in the rural Veneto and had come to music through the Church. He had been sent to study in Venice where after sampling the city's artistic delights he had jumped his ecclesiastical ship and joined the household of a wealthy patron of culture. There he had organised musical entertainments while consuming volumes of literature and history from the nobleman's extensive library.

Although Lorenzo was musically talented, it appeared that his real love was Italian literature. In Lisbon he gave classes in a fashionable picture gallery which were to his frustration attended by people acquiring the gloss of culture rather than artistic appreciation. When Lorenzo spoke about his passion for the language and its beauties, the mask of comfortable assurance slipped a little. A bitter edge could be heard in his sardonic mockery of polite society. Yet the Poet recited and interpreted the Italian classics rather than compose his own work. That was focused on the libretti which gave him a place in the city's thriving theatrical life.

As far as Flora could make out, the young Gozzi had left his patron's house in some kind of disgrace and had turned to the theatre as a way of earning. Venice offered every kind of stage entertainment, official and unofficial, but the opera was the most lavish and prosperous of the arts in a city that valued spectacle above all else. Except, in Lorenzo's mordant judgement, secrecy and disguise. He had fallen into writing a libretto by chance, and discovered that his scattered talents suited what he called 'that peculiar half-breed form, trapped between music and literature'. This fortunate knack had in due course launched his career and taken him across Europe wherever Italian opera was performed.

According to Lorenzo, Vienna was the capital of musical culture, and the scene of his greatest success. At the same time he admitted that he had no idea why some productions had succeeded and others failed. For himself, he had no control over the final presentation of an opera and was often bemused by the fickleness of audiences. The trick was to keep playing a different hand till the right cards came up. Contacts and persuasion were all. It was apparent that Lorenzo could be charming when he chose.

It was not clear how long Gozzi had stayed in Vienna or why he had left his Mecca, other than like Flora to experience Lisbon's famous new theatre. At the same time his work here seemed to cause him little effort and to offer even less satisfaction. Perhaps the Poet too was enjoying a period of calm after troubled times. One day he might tell her that story, if he chose.

It was an autumn evening when Flora had lingered at the Miradouro to watch the last embers of sunset. As she made her way down past the Cathedral, darkness had gathered in the narrow streets and the interiors were lit. To reach Villa Flor she had to turn left and make a slow ascent back towards Rua de São Pedro.

There was a small square at the start of the Rua where the winding routes from each side of the Cathedral joined and a tavern spilled out amidst a few gnarled trees. It was a popular drinking place in the Alfama, and Flora pulled her shawl over her head to hurry past. But the glow of light from inside drew her eye. It was like an illuminated stage – tables, faces, bottles emerald and ruby. And sitting alone to one side was Lorenzo.

She stood for a moment compelled. He had no wig, but unevenly cut grey hair receded from his brow. You could not mistake those strong features. But the face was haggard and sunk. The table was littered with empty bottles. He was in a soiled waistcoat and stared downwards oblivious to the crowd around him. Flora forced herself to look away and walk by.

She went to her room in the Villa yard and took no part in the social meal that evening. The next day Gozzi did not appear at the theatre, nor was he at the cafe. Flora prepared her evening meal as normal, dressed her hair and tidied the little room, checking that all her personal treasures were safely in the box inside her canvas bag below the bed. Then she went across the walkway.

When she knocked the voice told her to come in. Lorenzo was standing in his room by a table at the window. He was pale but freshly shaven, relaxed in his compact frame and upright stance. He was wearing a white shirt and britches. He looked and spoke her name, Flora, without surprise or emphasis. She moved towards him and he opened his arms to welcome and enfold her in his strength.

Flora's change in life was quickly accepted by the community of the Villa. People appreciated her modest way of dealing with them in the daily round, but there was an underlying belief that Flora carried some distinction about with her. Renata sometimes used her whole name, Flora McIvor, in mysterious intimation of this. Becoming the Poet's companion and mistress confirmed what had always been generally known.

The only practical issue arose around food. As part of her campaign to install Ligia officially in the old apartments, with full marital status, Mãe had been organising a constant flow of dishes which were delivered morning and evening by her fair assistant. Ligia herself avoided the smelly, messy business of cooking whenever possible. Flora however ate very simply avoiding the rich fish sauces which were the staple of Alfama cuisine, and Lorenzo, who seemed to take little interest in food, was quickly converted to her preference for fresh produce lightly cooked in the local olive oil.

At first Ligia threatened a scene but as she had no genuine interest in the Poet it was more scripted than delivered. Soon Renata called her off, for though she was disappointed that her first scheme had fallen through, she came to feel that bringing together Flora and the Poet had always been in her mind as an alternative possibility. The lustre still accrued to the credit of her establishment, and it left her the priest as an undisputed focus for her own affections.

For Flora those first weeks were a slow revelation as she and Lorenzo, long used to living by themselves, adjusted to each other's presence. He felt the quiet assurance of her daily patterning, her steady temperament, and the warmth of her touch. Apart from the months with Fergus at Castle McIvor, and the stresses of her time with Clementina, she had not experienced intimacy with anyone since early childhood. She felt something in her coming alive. She enjoyed his cultured conversation, wit and good humour, and her body responded to his pleasure in unexpected ways.

The days and weeks went by with no change to the couple's working routines. In the mornings Flora still rose early to shop and prepare food for the day ahead. She took Lorenzo coffee and left him in bed with books and papers spread around him. This he promised was the most productive time for writing. They always spoke briefly to each other at the theatre, but Flora left him to hold court at the cafe in the afternoons, so that she could finish work as soon as the performance was underway.

The big difference was their coming together each evening to eat and share the last hours of the day. Lorenzo's frank delight in her broke down a long cultivated reserve. Something on the heart lifted, releasing her at last to speak about Glengarry.

But to let Lorenzo understand that calamity, she had to explain the McIvor inheritance, the clans in Scotland and the Jacobite struggle. For the first time she spoke openly about Fergus' death, Clementina, and the conspiracy to abduct the royal family in London. He listened to the whole account in attentive astonished silence until she reached her last word.

'It's like a novel, Flora, in which you have survived every chapter. Surely you must write about this and tell your story? They say that novels are the coming thing.'

'No, Lorenzo, don't speak of it in that way. I do not have an artist's freedom to tell. I must not attract any interest to myself. Palazzo Muti's tentacles stretch across Europe. I have barely escaped that past and must not give it any hold on us.'

'Poor girl, you have been living all this time in fear of discovery.'

Flora was surprised by his focus on her secret life, rather than Glengarry's betrayal, which was what she most needed to share. 'I had to tell you, Lorenzo, about the man who abused my trust. If there is to be no concealment between us.'

Lorenzo shrugged. 'Dearest, dear Flora, my love. Life is full of such betrayals. We should not let them stain our souls or our freedom to embrace.' And he took her in his arms, and she gave way and wept and was comforted. So great was her relief that she did not look for any revelations in return.

There were still periods in which Lorenzo's underlying discontents broke out. His mood altered and sought release in drinking. Flora did not try to staunch that bitter flow but to divert it, encouraging him to drink at home and to take some food. Sometimes she pulled his insensible body over to the bed to let him sleep off the ill effects, without the dangers to which drunkenness in the Alfama taverns could lead.

The next morning she would leave him sleeping heavily, and in the evening resume their normal conversation without comment or reproach. Lorenzo would look apologetic for an instant, and then he too picked up where they had left off, as if nothing had happened to disturb the even tenor of their way.

One evening after such an episode, Flora stumbled unintentionally into an antidote to Lorenzo's nagging complaint.

'Did you ever hear Rameau's Amorous Indies, Lorenzo?'

'No, but I know it is popular in Paris.'

'Very popular. The music is beautiful, and the subject has great appeal. But the libretto is thin. Could you not write for a new production in Lisbon? You have influence at the opera. Rameau's librettist, Fuselier used to come to the Palais Royal. He revered the composer's memory and would not allow any changes to the words he had used.'

'What is the story?'

'That is the trouble. There are several different stories, poorly expressed in words at least. Yet the theme is love in exotic places, and every world with which Lisbon trades from Constantinople to the Americas is represented. The quays here are loaded with the produce of these distant worlds, and filled with faces of India, Africa and America. The subject is crying out for a poetry of amour to match the old master's music. I made new costumes in Paris but what pictures we could make here where the colours are already present to the public eye.'

Lorenzo again looked at Flora as if she had drawn back the curtains from some wholly unexpected design.

'I wonder if there is a copy of the old libretto in Lisbon?'

'I have one in my trunk. Would you like to read it?'

Within a fortnight he had crafted a new script working between the original French, Italian, and the score which he had found at Teatro São Carlos. As both musician and poet, Lorenzo was in his element, interweaving much more closely the four love stories through language as Rameau had harmonised them in sound. Then began his campaign to have a new production mounted.

As the labyrinthine theatrical politics played out, Flora looked again at the sketches she had drawn for François Bouchier in Paris. They were stowed away neglected in the old trunk, which had now travelled across the walkway to the apartment. She realised that much more was possible for her in Lisbon. The theatre could provide new scenery for each Act. The style of costuming here was already more naturalised than at the Palais. In addition the huge Mercado by the new port contained, alongside the fruits and spices of the world, rich silks and brocades from the east, dyed woollen fabrics from the Americas, an abundance of feathers, decorated leatherwork and other adornments There were even fabrics made from rushes and bark. Quietly as the manoeuvrings went on over the backers, musicians and singers, she was steadily accumulating new materials.

What finally swung São Carlos behind Amorous Indies was the dance sequences. Since the house generally followed Italian tradition, an expanded troupe, sequentially costumed in a variety of native exotics, was judged to be bold innovation and sure box office. Flora's new drawings played a decisive part in winning the merchants' support, as Lorenzo fulsomely acknowledged.

For the first time, Lorenzo and Flora shared their creative work as well as daily life. They were both at full stretch, as Flora brought in extra costume makers and moved between the scene painters and the cutting room. Lorenzo sat in on all the rehearsals arguing publicly with the music director while advising each singer discreetly on phrasing and expression. When not in rehearsal he gave extra lessons and appeared in all the fashionable gathering places to promote Amorous Indies as the theatrical event of the season, if not of many seasons. Now a rebuilt, rejuvenated Lisbon could outclass venerable Paris.

And so it proved. The opening night was everything its devisers hoped for, and more. That elusive alchemy of success worked its magic on performers and audience alike. Encores and standing ovations followed one upon the other until eventually the curtain had to be lowered and the crowd spilled out into a perfect starlit night. As celebrations continued in the town, Flora eventually managed to tug an exhausted but exhilarated Lorenzo away from the throng towards home.

The courtyard was deserted and peaceful. In the apartment they undressed like peasants who had spent every daylight hour in backbreaking toil, and lay down joined hip to hip in resignation and content. Soon they fell together into deep dreamless slumber.

The first free day after the opening of Amorous Indies was as usual a Monday. Flora lingered at home, and when Lorenzo got up he announced that they should go on an outing to celebrate. He proceeded to dress in his finest wear and encouraged Flora to change out of her workaday clothes.

Early morning rain bursts had been chasing each other over the estuary, but the skies had cleared to a crystal bright morning as they left Villa Flor and climbed towards the Miradouro. However Lorenzo did not delay to enjoy the view. He continued up towards the Castelo and then bearing right below the fortress walls, he and Flora strolled arm in arm into a part of the city she did not know. It was less crowded with open squares and newer apartments than Alfama. Soon they came out into a broad piazza that swept up to an imposing church.

'São Vicente de Fora. Come, there is something I want to show you.'

Instead of starting the ascent up a grand stair towards

the ceremonial entrance, Lorenzo guided Flora to one side where the rise was less steep. They went through a shaded archway into a side chamber of Paradise. It was a courtyard longer than broad, with a pillared portico on three walls. In the centre was an ornamental garden with small trees, flowers and bushes in a sequence of raised beds. On the right hand side a cascade of pure water tumbled into a brimming pool from which streams spilled over and ran in channels through the garden. The whole portico was tiled in the intense primary colours of Lisbon's sun and sea. Flora stood entranced by its vivid beauty.

'What is this place?'

'A monastery, and the burial crypt of Portugal's kings and queens. But wait here till I see if the priest is ready.'

'A priest?'

'Yes, dear Flora, for our wedding.'

'Lorenzo. I am not prepared, dressed…'

'But you will marry me? Come, sit here by the fountain.'

She sat obediently and listened to the water splash and flow. It was inevitable like a dream. An elderly priest appeared with Lorenzo and took them through a small door into the immense gloom of the church. There in a side chapel he conducted the brief ceremony, and taking them back to the courtyard departed with a blessing. Then they went for lunch near the Castelo and home to rest.

The couple continued as before, but Flora felt as if some deeper level of trust had been reached, even as Lorenzo basked amidst the bustle of theatrical plaudits. She was grateful that after so many journeys, her life had found a safe harbour, while she took pleasure in her husband's success. She began to go sometimes to the ancient Cathedral and make her devotion again after so many years to Jesu of the Sacred Heart and to Our Lady. She thought of Clementina and prayed that she and her daughter Louisa might be unharmed, secure in their love. And she prayed for the soul of Fergus, pleading the intercession of Saint Teresa.

Some few weeks later, after an unprecedented run Amorous Indies was coming to its triumphant close. She came back early to the Villa to find Lorenzo already in the apartment. He was very quiet, at the table, staring out towards the sea. There were no papers or books around him. She went on with her normal tasks, tidying and getting things ready for the evening meal.

'Flora, could you sit down for a moment.'

She sat in the chair on the other side and folded her hands on the table. He did not touch her or look at her face.

'There is part of my life I have not told you about.'

'Tell me now then, Lorenzo.' She reached out a hand across towards him but his gaze had fastened on the polished surface.

'After I was in Vienna, I returned to Venice. There was a friend of mine there from childhood in the countryside, Girolamo Michele. His dream was to take control of a theatre, not an opera house but a comedy house playing Goldoni. Like me he was brought up with nothing except hunger. He said it was the only kind of theatre that made money; that I could direct the actors and music, while he ran the business. He was caught up in his plan, like a child with a toy castle, and convinced me to give him all the money I had.'

Lorenzo paused and drew breath.

'For a while things seemed to go well. Our productions were acclaimed, but the theatre was decrepit, always needing repairs, and in truth audiences wanted a change from Goldoni. Yet Girolamo refused to consider failure. When I gave him the money, we signed a deed of partnership, but as losses mounted without my knowledge, he sold half of the building to a member of the nobility, and then borrowed money on security of the whole property. Before things finally collapsed, Girolamo fled the city, telling me that he was going to sell a vineyard which he had been left by an old uncle in the Veneto.

Somehow I still trusted him, perhaps because at heart he believed in his own falsehoods. They were much more appealing than the truth. Is that not the secret of all theatre?'

For a moment he looked at Flora, but she was intent on following his story to the end, as if compelled by some malign spell.

'When the creditors foreclosed I was liable for half of all the debts, which were owed twice. No-one it seemed had been paid at the theatre for two months. When he realised that Girolamo had disappeared, the moneylender took out a contract on his life as Venetians do. I was imprisoned awaiting trial, but a lady whom I knew well at the theatre came to visit me bringing food and spare clothes – a woman's dress, cape and hat. She remained in the cell till I had escaped disguised in her garments. I managed to flee the city, outlawed and penniless.'

'What happened to her?'

'Girolamo is certainly dead. They will have found him. As for that brave woman, I don't know. I got out of Italy, travelling as a beggar, and have severed all connection with my home city. Until today.'

'Today? What do you mean?'

'This afternoon a man came to the theatre asking for me by name. He left an address. But I saw him approaching from my seat in the cafe, and I knew him immediately as a Venetian man of business. He has come to collect the debt, or my life. I should not have put my name to our opera.'

'Can we not pay? I have money in my box.' She started to get up but Lorenzo pulled her back.

'It is a large sum of money, Flora. Listen now, for our lives' sake. This is what we must do. I have booked passage on a ship leaving tomorrow for New York in America. Fortunately I have the money from Amorous Indies. You must remain here, for a time. That man will soon find this place. Tell him when he comes that I have gone to Paris to arrange another production of my libretto, and that you expect me back in two months. Then you should stay, working as normal until he gives up watching. In two or three months you can come and join me in New York. Have you enough money to do that?'

'Yes, but what kind of place is New York? Is there not war between the French and the English?'

'Yes, there has been fighting but not in New York. It was a Dutch port till Britain took it and drove away the Indians. The English are at war with France and Spain for possession of the Americas. They do not like Europeans, Flora, even though they want our music and literature. That is why it is the best place to go. No-one will find us there.'

'Can I live here alone?'

'You did before. You can, Flora. You are stronger than you know. Forgive me for bringing this unhappiness. I thought I had escaped Venice but their web spins far. We will be reunited. I shall not forget or abandon you for a moment. You are my wife.'

He held both her hands in his but she could not keep still, or take in anything further.

'I must pack your trunk. There is washing in the courtyard.'

'Don't go outside. Ligia will bring it in. Please, prepare some food, and I will gather my books. Who knows, New

York may bring us better fortune.'

'What could be better than the life we share here, Lorenzo?'

He did not answer but turned away towards the bed where Flora could see the trunk open and already half full.

Eventually, Flora went to bed, tossing and turning in restless sleep. Lorenzo seemed to stay up all night unable to surrender his anxious watch. As first light crept through their windows he embraced Flora and slipped out to be early at the quay ready for boarding. She turned away from the windows and shrank into herself. She could not comprehend what had happened. Tears would not come to her aid.

Things transpired exactly as Lorenzo had foretold. Looking back, Flora was amazed at his cool head in the face of danger. First the black coated man reappeared at Teatro São Carlos asking for Maestro Gozzi. Two days later, he came enquiring at Villa Flor, and finally arrived at the apartment door.

'Does Lorenzo Gozzi live here?'

'Yes, but he is away from home at present.'

'Who are you?'

'His wife.'

'So you know where he is?'

'Yes, of course, he has gone to Paris, to try and repeat his success with the Rameau opera.'

'Are you telling me the truth?'

'Why would I tell you anything else? The whole of Lisbon knows of my husband's success with The Amorous Indies.'

The man's brow darkened and he turned away without acknowledgement or thanks.

'Shall I say who called?'

'Tell him that Girolamo Michele needs him in Venice,' was shouted back up the stair, 'He has not been forgotten.'

Over succeeding days she felt watched. But Mãe Renata was more than a match for any surveillance, and once inside Villa Flor she was surrounded by friends. No-one in the theatre or the Alfama was surprised that the Poet had gone on the back of his success to seek more fame in Paris, and as Lorenzo was not in the city no sighting or encounter could upset that version of events.

However as the weeks passed Flora felt a need to share her troubling secret with someone, so she confided in Renata. In any case, how was she to manage her own departure without arousing suspicion? Mãe drank in the tale with ravenous eyes, but her first instinct was to pull the delicately formed Flora to her full heart and squeeze the breath from the slighter woman's body.

'Don't be afraid. The Poet is an honourable man and he will wait for you. As for that Venetian I will set the stonecutter on him like a dog. Now that Jaimhino and Ligia are betrothed, he will do anything for me. See, do not cry. Why was the Poet so foolish, but now he has you to look out for. He is your husband. It will all be fine, I promise. Have you money for your passage? Good, than I will go to reserve for you, so no-one can notice you are leaving. But please come and eat with us again in the court. Do not be alone in these days, for friends are all around you.'

It was too much for an exhausted Flora. She wept, and Mãe wept in sympathy. She was relieved that Renata showed such faith in Lorenzo, rather than casting doubt or worse adding new revelations. The strain of these lonely weeks had taken their toll.

Mãe however was as good as her word, watching

carefully over Flora, and booking passage for her on an American ship, the Columbia. There had been no further sign of the black coated man, so Flora packed up her life at Villa Flora into two large canvas bags and prepared to depart, telling everyone other than Renata that she was following Lorenzo to Paris. On a misty autumn morning she rose before dawn and crossing the walkway went down into the courtyard. Mãe was waiting by the well with a further basket full of food and a huge shawl which she wrapped round Flora's shoulders.

'You will need this for a blanket on the ship.'

Then she pushed Flora out of the gate, and for the last time she went down the steep Alfama steps to the port, where in the deeper harbourage the three-masted Colombia waited, her drooping sails swathed with early morning fog.

Later, when Flora was reunited with Lorenzo in New York, she found it hard to distinguish his memories of the voyage from her own. Both crossings had taken more than two months and had been accomplished in the face of constant headwinds and gales. Life on board was equally a battle against cold, sickness and hunger. Mãe's blanket had been a godsend, while Lorenzo had not reckoned on having to provide bedding. He had resorted to using his complete stock of garments as a compendious mattress and blanket.

The food supplies ran short after a fortnight. Flora's bundle included cheese and meal. Lorenzo talked his way into the captain's rough cabin where the ship's only reliable supplies of wine and liquor staved off hunger. Meanwhile pigs and hens ran about midships in cacophonous terror. Those which were not swept overboard were slaughtered in the worst of conditions to provide the basis of the galley's poor imitation of cookery. Flora avoided these greasy slops, suspicious that many of the retchings blamed on seasickness had a more immediate cause.

There were only two women aboard the ship so their shared worm eaten niche, which contained four slatted bunks, became Flora's refuge. It offered shelter along with a place to sleep and store her precious bags. The other woman, a Spaniard, was also travelling to join her husband, but spent most of the voyage incoherent with sea sickness.

Lorenzo's bunk was in the lower passenger deck where lighter items of cargo were stored. He slept there fitfully in an open bunk, as if in a poorhouse, but spent most of his time drinking and gambling in a vain attempt to shut out the driving grey rain soaked winds which ceaselessly roused up the big seas.

Nonetheless, after the blur of those weeks, Flora's clearest memory was of the approach from open ocean to the Hudson river estuary. It reminded her of the mighty Tagus and its narrow sea gate within which Lisbon sheltered beside its open expanse of water. The day was clear with a rare following breeze and as if to welcome the weary Colombia, dolphins and seals swam alongside, while the air was filled with raucous cries of gulls. The ship nosed into the bay and made good headway past an island with a ruined fort till the two forks of the huge river were visible, and between them the port of New York on the tip of Manhattan Island.

Flora felt light headed and dizzy as the ship nosed into its berth. Passengers and their luggage were manhandled down the gangplank onto a quay that seemed to sway with every race and condition of humanity. Porters yelled at the latest arrivals, competing for business and jostling those who had come to welcome the ship. She clutched her bags tightly, desperate to escape the crowd and find her own way to the town. But on the edge of the crowd she heard her name called out. There was the familiar compact figure, paler, grey hair pulled back in a pigtail, but wearing his usual ironic yet appreciative smile. She collapsed into her husband's welcoming embrace.

Lorenzo steered her out of the docks and through the busy streets to a rooming house where there was fresh milk and bread to eat, and a comfortable bed in which Flora would sink finally into motionless sleep. As she lay allowing her husband's comfortable tones to wash over her brow, she was able for the first time since their sudden separation to admit a future. Now the voyage had ended in this way, she could surely leave the last months behind like a bad dream or episode of fever, and begin life afresh in this new world.

The next day she woke to noise. It rose up from the street and filled all the space around her bed. The clatter of wheels on rutted road. The cries of traders and street hucksters. A background hum of grinding and mending. Even the narrow skies seemed to press in at the window. For an instant she saw the vista of blue stretching out from their apartment in Villa Flor. She heard the early morning quiet before Alfama came to life. But she was alone in a world that raucously demanded remorseless attention.

Lorenzo returned shortly with bread rolls and coffee from a nearby bakery. He sat on the edge of the bed and passed over a warm cup and pieces of roll dipped in honey. As Flora reached out from her blankets she felt the cold air on her skin.

'Are you able to get up?'

'Yes, I'm fine, just tired.'

'We'll go and look round the town. It takes a few days to recover from that hellish crossing.'

They stepped out together into the street, retracing their steps back towards the port. She felt the raw cold like a blow to her face, and was amazed how, staggering in her exhaustion from the ship, she had barely noticed the temperature. Had that been only yesterday? The people hurrying through crowded streets wore every kind of garment against the cold – furs, skins and horse blankets alongside the coats and cloaks of the more prosperous. There were African faces as there had been at Lisbon, a huge variety of Europeans, a few Asiatics and the occasional brown skinned native with plaited hair and feathers, stepping proudly through the mêlée.

The narrow street was packed with shops each of which had an outside stall displaying its wares. Then suddenly it ended in a large open space on the other side of which could be seen the walled harbour and beside it a substantial fort. This had been the first armed colonial outpost, originally Dutch and now British. However Lorenzo turned back without comment and headed in the direction they had come by another street identical to the first.

Flora could see now how brick built orderly houses at the foot quickly gave way to mixtures of brick and wood, and finally to haphazard timber construction. The layout too became more disorderly with streets crisscrossing and bending in different directions. It all depended, Lorenzo explained, on how each section of the original land had been purchased and then variously developed, lacking any overall plan. Yet an overwhelming energy filled the place. People hurried about intent on their business. And everywhere the rowdiness of making and selling was at full pitch. Eventually the houses began to thin out and the streets trailed past fields, orchards and finally into open farmland. Even in its frozen state the country came to Flora as a welcoming relief.

However, once more, Lorenzo was disinclined to linger in the cold and they retraced their route into the town. Heading most of the way back towards the port, he turned into a road he called Wall Street and stopped at the sign of the Tontine Coffee House. Inside was warm and rich smelling, and though the place seemed packed with traders and merchants, they found a side bench to squeeze into on their own and ordered coffee. When the drinks came in steaming cups they sipped the heat gratefully and looked about them.

'It's the best place I have found here,' he commented.

'A little piece of Europe, perhaps.'

'Until you hear the talk. It is all trade or politics, yet good for my English. Though there are French and a few Italians and Dutch, even Spanish, it is mainly English here.'

That explained the harshness of the street voices. Though the tones were not the same as the speech of London. This was an entirely new place, for Flora at least.

'And Scots,' Lorenzo continued,' there are many Scottish here, and on the Canadian frontier.'

'What can we do?'

'There is no theatre or opera, Flora. Occasionally some English actors but the mood here is against England. They want more freedom for their provinces, perhaps a new country.'

'Then there may be bloodshed. I thought I had left that behind me.'

'The British fight in Canada, but there is no war here. Everything is trade and that is how we should look to live.'

'How, Lorenzo, what do you mean?'

'We must rent a shop, not by the port but near the edges where new, better houses are being built. Soon there will be one place for the poor, downtown as they say, and another for the prosperous where there is space and light in the summer at least.'

'Trading what?'

'You, my dear, will be New York's finest dressmaker. I shall deal in printed books. Until we can see better days for civilised manners.'

'You think they will buy new dresses and literature?'

'To begin with it will be hard, patching and mending, but this city is growing in wealth and soon people will desire the finer things in life. We must be patient. One day they will have a concert hall, theatre and even the opera.'

Flora found it hard to match this prediction to the streets she had walked with Lorenzo that morning.

'I will do my best,' she agreed, 'but will we live above the shop?'

'For now, we have no choice. We shall have to put money down.'

'I hope we have enough, but there is one thing I need to ask for, Lorenzo. There must be some quiet where we live. I cannot survive with the noise that surrounds the rooms we are in. I have always had some quiet for my refuge.'

'I understand, though as a child I longed for the din of Venice. But as I say, Flora, we will go out from the downtown to where it is more peaceful, and cheaper. But business will grow there, I wager on it.'

'Please, let us be done with gambling and live plainly.'

'Here, my dear one, there is only plain living unless you drink hard liquor and go to a whorehouse. Look, I have these bills of lease. We should go today to see their shops. My money is almost gone.'

'Yes, but first I must go back and rest, just for an hour or two. My sea legs will not manage another long walk. Come and keep me company, Lorenzo, for a time. We can pretend to siesta even without sunshine or lunch.'

The old smile came back for the first time that day. She saw he was more troubled than his plan pretended.

'You bring the sunshine back for me, dear one. I was unsure that you would come. Without you it is not worth the struggle for me to make a new life. But now you are here, everything can be done.'

By that evening they had paid the deposit on a dilapidated clapboard building on the north edge of the town where new streets were advancing daily into the countryside.

Everything proved harder. The house was bitterly cold. It cost all of Flora's remaining coins to make it habitable and to provide scant starting stock for the new dressmaking business. Moreover it was a long time since she had made clothes for present day fashions. Most of the women in New York wore working clothes or eked out some imported garments. So her main jobs were low cost repairs. Only gradually did Flora get a feel for what might sell as new, and adapt her designs to the market.

Lorenzo proved an excellent promoter, getting cards printed and distributed in town. He also hit on the idea that they should collect the repairs and have the finished work delivered by a messenger. In New York time was money. But his biggest breakthrough came when he managed to buy on credit the library of a deceased clergyman, whose catholic tastes had ranged far beyond protestant theology. Education and reading were in favour, and in the absence of theatre or a concert hall, they were the main sources of cultural life.

The drawback of bookselling however was that New York by itself was not yet a large enough marketplace. Lorenzo had to travel by coach to New Jersey and as far as Philadelphia buying and selling in order to turnover his stock. The roads and inns were execrable making these journeys a misery, while Flora dreaded the trips when she was left alone to face the drudgery of her daily routine. Without her husband's presence, she mind brooded over what had been lost and could not see beyond the unfulfilling grind. Would they never be able to go back to Europe?

For the first time she became aware of stiffening joints, and the grey streaks appearing in hair that had been as black and glossy as a raven's wing. However, Lorenzo would return full of complaints but also claiming modest successes. She was sceptical when he talked up the future, yet his presence lifted her spirits.

In reality, Lorenzo's business was growing, and when the more aspiring citizens established a university in New York, he was well placed to supply its new library. These contacts also resulted in the proposal to establish a concert society. There was already the basis of an occasional orchestra in the town combining music teachers with some skilled amateurs, but his plan was to mount a season of performances. Progress on this proposal was slow, but again the foundation of Colombia University provided an opportunity.

Lorenzo kept Flora abreast of every bit of progress, and the reverses, in his efforts to recoup something of their artistic initiative. She realised that he was actively trying to involve her in an effort to relieve the frequent depressions. In his own way he was more attentive to her than when they had lived so contentedly in Lisbon, and she was touched by this affection.

As things improved they hired a seamstress to under-take the routine jobs. She was an old negro woman called Bessie, who had been freed by her master in Georgia and managed to reach New York. Flora began to do more fittings in the shop and occasionally in people's homes nearby. The warm summer brought happier times to mind, and in the fall Flora could walk out of an evening into the countryside to admire the colours on the trees and the abundance of fruit in the orchards.

She was pleased and surprised when one day that autumn Lorenzo returned from the port with a book for her.

'It's a translation by Melchiore Cesarotti of some Scottish work. I knew Cesarotti a bit in Venice. He loved the theatre but was an enemy of Goldoni. This is poetry though.'

'Can I keep it to read?'

'I got it for you. It was in a shipment of French and Italian books for the university but no-one here will know of it. They want Dante and Petrarch.'

That night she sat up late accompanied by a candle, and balancing on her nose glass frames that Lorenzo had purchased to help her eyes with finer needlework. The Poems of Ossian by James MacPherson was a compelling yet puzzling read, in Cesarotti's Italian at least. His lyrical descriptions evoked the atmosphere of the Scottish mountains, but the stories, such as they were, bore small resemblance to any of the tales and legends she had heard in her childhood or at Castle McIvor.

MacPherson's Fingal was obviously Fionn the martial Gaelic hero, but who was Temora and why was everyone in the poems permanently lamenting? Many of the stories of Fionn and his warrior band as she remembered them were fantastic and humorous, not mournful. She felt that the author was trying to represent the Gaelic world to a European audience rather than his own people. Now his book was here in America, in Italian and presumably in

English as well.

The next morning she quizzed Lorenzo for any clues to understanding the work.

'Apparently MacPherson's book is a great success in Britain and is being translated into all the languages.' This seemed to be all that Lorenzo knew about Ossian.

'But it is a dream vision of his own making; it is not Scotland,' Flora objected.

'There is a new movement in letters, Flora, away from the natural. Your MacPherson may be a man of the new age.'

'He is certainly writing out of defeat and despair. The massacres after Culloden were devastating for our people, and he is a Highlander. Yet I could relate the story of Ossian better than MacPherson does. His treatment is like Fuselier's version of the Americas in Amorous Indies. There is no flesh or blood.'

Lorenzo showed more interest at the mention of his rewriting triumph.

'Why don't you recollect the story and we could make a libretto?'

'For whom? We have no opera house.'

'But, Flora, when the concert society begins we can perform some operatic pieces without costume or scenery. It was sometimes done this way in Vienna.'

'That is serving pasta without the sauce.'

'Better eat pasta than starve.'

'Alright, let me make notes and write some passages. But you would have to turn the action into drama for music.'

'I will need your help. This could be New York's first opera. Your Highlanders can stand for the Indians. Are they not the natives here?'

'So we shall need costumes, and feathers!'

Flora did not truly believe in Lorenzo's operatic project.

The concert society was not yet established despite endless discussions. Yet she snatched at the chance to recover something of what they had shared in Lisbon.

She began by outlining in her mind the life of Ossian. That was a story that MacMurrough the bard had delighted in, and constantly repeated in the long rainy afternoons when there was no alternative diversion. He seemed to claim Ossian as a kind of patron saint of poets, so justifying frequent recitations of the birth, deeds, and fantastical wanderings of this first of bards. As Flora recalled, Ossian had gone to dwell with his love in a land without time or death beneath the sea, until overcome by longing for his native soil he had returned and crumbled into dust. At least Flora recalled the tale, or most of it, and she found that writing it down helped fill the gaps. Things started with Ossian's strange birth.

Fionn was out hunting one day and his hounds pursued a scent. When he caught up with them in a thicket they were gently licking instead of mauling a graceful hind. 'That is strange,' thought Fionn, 'it is as if this creature were trying to reach my fortress.' So they released the hind which went in front of the hunting party till they reached home. In the middle of that night there came to Fionn's bedside the most beautiful young women he had ever seen, slender and dark. 'Am I dreaming?' asked Fionn. 'No,' the woman said, 'I have escaped through the kindness of your hounds from a curse of the Grey One, who wished to possess me. Now I can be yours.' 'What is your name?' 'I am called Saba,' she replied.

From that time Fionn lived only for the lovely Saba, till his warriors grumbled and muttered against their leader's neglect of war. Eventually he had to leave in order to repel an invasion by the Norsemen. But when he returned Saba had gone, lured away by a dark stranger who had appeared in the shape of Fionn. For seven years he sought his lost love across land and sea, till one day his hounds ran down a strange quarry, which instead of killing they defended against all comers. It was a human child, a boy, who said he had lived in the forest mothered by a hind, until he had been driven away by a dark man. Neither Saba nor the Grey One were ever seen again, but the child was named Ossian, 'little fawn', and grew under Fionn's protection to become a poet of the Fianna.

This was the Ossian to whom James MacPherson ascribed the poems he had gathered. Could they belong to a bardic tradition of which MacMurrough had been unaware? More practically, who was the Grey Man and what dark hold did he have over Saba? That would need to be explained if any dramatic plot was to make sense.

It seemed unlikely that something could be fashioned from this material for the stage. Would there be a Rameau in America, and if such a talent emerged could he be persuaded to abandon MacPherson's plaintive siren in favour of such primitive old stories? Why would Scotland and its ancient struggles be of interest in this new world?

But Lorenzo's faith in America's future was unbounded, certainly able to embrace a magical tale that could have come from the forests of New England. Everything would be possible in such a land of opportunity and plenty, in time. For now he would prepare a libretto from the material. What other stories could Flora remember and write down? Would she not sketch scenery and costumes? One day they would realise their joint conception here and eventually take it back to Europe.

For now the daily grind of business must continue. Yet somehow an incipient dark had receded. Flora rose to work lighter in hand and heart. Lorenzo took up his campaign for the concert society with renewed vigour.

In late autumn a season of storms came on, sweeping away the last ragged leaves. Lorenzo left on an extended tour of his trading outposts before the full onset of winter closed the roads. Because of her husband's absence Flora was more frequently downtown, buying fabrics and settling accounts. Ever growing resentment against the taxes and restrictions of the colonial administration had made the atmosphere in New York tense throughout the summer heat. Flora almost welcomed the calmer mood that the winter freeze would of necessity bring.

One blustery morning she left the seamstress and an idle message boy in charge of the shop. She wanted to check the last cargos of the season at the port, for sometimes stray rolls of cloth could be bought cheaply in the sheds. She also needed to stretch her legs after the recent stormbound days, and enjoy a wan sun which was blinking through chasing clouds. Soon she was past the Tontine, over the denuded square which was the borderland between New York and the British garrison, and through the dock gates.

She turned left towards the wharves and walked down between long rows of open-sided sheds, looking out for the bays where unloaded goods were piled ready for shipment or collection. One whole section seemed to be full of people sheltering from the wind. They must be recent arrivals. Flora stopped. People of all ages were huddling together under blankets, between piles of baggage, but there was no hiding the tartan plaids. Highlanders. Fifty, maybe sixty, and some clearly distressed. She moved under the roof where the stench of dank misery filled her nostrils. She touched the first person she reached. The woman looked up from hollowed eyes.'

'Scottish?'

'Scotland. Nan Gaidheal. We are sick.'

Suddenly a bowed figure close by rose out of his blanket and stepped towards Flora. Gaunt, grey-haired but unmistakable.

'Nighean Ivor, mo cridhe. Mo cridhe, nighean McIvor.'

He went down on his knees and put his arms round her skirts.

'Calum. Tha Flora, nighean Ivor. Calum, it is really you.'

She stood for what seemed a long time as the bowed Highlander held her, and tears ran down her cheeks. Eventually she gently lifted Calum to his feet and walked with him towards the group which was shifting and turning towards this unexpected meeting.

'What has happened, Calum? Please in English.'

'These are Glengarry's people. They are being driven out by their chief. We were sailing to Canada but great storms are putting us here for a time. Many are sick from the long voyage and the winds and wet. Three months we have been at sea and hungry.'

'Yes, I understand. We will fetch food and more blankets. But why are you here?'

Calum looked away.

'I am married on a McDonell, a woman of Glen Garry. See, my wife, Catriona, and our children.'

A shawled woman came forward and bowed to Flora. She looked exhausted. A little boy, and even smaller girl, clung to her side, staring up at the stranger.

'Enough, for now, Calum, I will ask all your news, but first I must get food. Is there nowhere else you can go other than this shed?'

'They told us to wait here till the ship is once more ready.'

Flora hurried back through the town. Taking all the money she had in the house, she hired a cart and going to the nearest provisions merchant she had it loaded up with ham, bread, cheese, fruit and ale. The merchant was used to supplying out of town farmers and also had blankets in stock. She bought three large rolls of them and piled them up on the front of the wagon. Finally she purchased an iron brazier and firewood. The carter loaded them at the rear and secured the backboard. Then he climbed up beside Flora and they set off at a trot for the port.

If Flora had appeared as St Nicholas in person, she could not have been more a welcome visitant to that forlorn shed. Urged on by an excited Calum, the Highlanders were soon unloading, lighting the brazier and gathering round to share out desperately needed food. Yet despite their evident hunger, the old were brought forward first to be fed, then the children, and only last did the fitter adults eat. Some were unable to stand so a portion was taken to each until everyone had been given whatever they could manage to swallow.

Finally the ale was passed round, and a few bottles and flasks silently appeared from the baggage or the folds of plaids. Calum rose to bring Flora a dram, where she had been placed reluctantly at the seat of honour next the fire. He handed her a tin mug and she solemnly raised it to the assembled company. With a heartfelt 'Sláinte', an assortment of vessels were raised in concert and the whisky thrown back with a ceremonial flourish starkly at odds with their straitened situation.

As bodies warmed and the tension of hunger eased, people fell asleep. Others came back for more food and drink. For a few it was too much too soon, and the sounds of vomiting could be heard in the passages. Gradually the circle round the brazier thinned till by early evening

Calum and Flora were left together as the darkness gathered round.

'I cannot believe it is yourself. God has spared me for this sight.'

'I went to France with Clementina, Calum, and eventually to Portugal. We sailed from there to America, my husband Lorenzo and I. He is away inland trading in books.'

'The old king still lives in Rome. God save the king.'

'I believe so.'

'And Miss Clementina has a child by the prince, Duchess Louisa. She will be recognised and give birth to his heirs. So the royal blood will not be dying. The king will come back to his own.'

'But what of the McIvors, Calum?'

'The children of Ivor are shielded from the worst because Captain Waverley and the Lady Rose are watching over the Glen to prevent our destruction. But it is not the same without a chief. We are not allowed to wear the kilt or carry weapons or tune the pipes. The hall of Ivor is silent and chill. So I left and went to Glengarry. He was to raise the people again for the prince.'

'He was a traitor, Calum. Glengarry betrayed the prince. He betrayed Miss Clementina, and especially this daughter of Ivor.'

'We did not know then what we are knowing now. He is shamed by the betraying of his people. Glengarry has sold his own children as slaves for Sassenach gold. The Braes of Garry are emptied Miss Flora, and we his people must flee like hunted deer. We are seeking a new home in this land of Canada, if we can get there alive.'

Calum looked around at the sleeping huddles, listening for their groans and sighs.

'I will bring more food tomorrow, Calum.'

'Blessed be the daughter of Ivor. On the feast day of Bride she shall come from her hillock amidst the heather. I shall not touch her and she will not harm a single heel of the Gael.'

Flora bent her head, letting these gracious words settle amongst the embers.

'Calum, I would like to ask you about one of the old stories.' Calum sipped his dram and looked attentive. 'It's about Fionn and Ossian.' He nodded encouragingly. 'Why did the Grey One have such power over Saba and steal her and her child away from Fionn?'

'I am not the bard, Miss Flora.'

'But you are a storyteller.'

'Indeed, I know the stories. When Fionn Mac Cumhnail was young the northmen are capturing his oldest son. He went to Manaan Mac Lir, God of the seas, for help, but the God he would not give that help until Fionn brought him a cup of healing for his own child who was gravely sick. So Fionn sought the aid of a Druid whose knowledge is being both dark and deep. And in this way he gained the cup of healing, and freed his own son. But when all was done he did not remember to honour the Druid whose magic was so great. And he came in time as a Grey Magician to claim his revenge on Fionn. For surely, the Grey Ones can drain all colour from the world and leave but the shadow of life.'

'That makes sense. One story explains another.'

'There is always the story, Miss Flora, before the story.'

'And a cause. From disregard and denial comes the betrayal. Evil is not causeless for the one who destroys, without feeling or knowing what they do.'

'You are minding Glengarry. He is of that kind.'

'Yes, I think you are right. He felt neglected, in the shadow of his father and grandfather, his brother, even his brave cousin Lochgarry. But I fear him no longer. He has done his worst. In the end love is stronger than the indifference of death. Do you believe that, Calum?'

'My love for the McIvor has never died. He was the light of my eye.'

He took Flora's hand and touched her fingers gently with his mouth. She left her hand in his.

'Fergus is something we will always share, Calum. You have brought him back to me tonight, for which I give you my thanks and blessing.' It was Calum's turn to bow his head. 'Now it is late. I must go home and you will sleep. In the morning I shall bring more food, and we will see when this ship is to depart.'

At home Flora lay awake thinking over the day's turbulent events. That the McDonells should have been driven into New York by the autumn gales was extraordinary enough. But the chance of her finding them in this crowded place was beyond coincidence. Glengarry finally exposed – surely not unexpected, yet a relief. And to know that Clementina had won the unequal struggle for her daughter. That news made Flora's spirits sing.

Then there was Ossian whose art she knew proved stronger than the Grey Magician, even though Saba did not escape his enchantment. How to present such a figure? Suddenly she heard Glengarry's voice, its French softly accented with the softness of Gaelic. Fergus had spoken in the same way but with more emphasis; Alister Ruadh was lower pitched, more insidious. What was he saying? Nothing, only the sound of grey emptiness. Yet he had recalled Fergus to her. The image rose in her mind of a dark king of the dead masked in gold and silver. Where had she seen that picture? She could hear the music rising in an underworld of her mind. Dreaming.

Flora slept late but felt unrested. She went to the exchange and drew a bill of credit on her stock. Then she hired two carts and went back to another larger store for provisions. This would give the clan enough for the voyage and the inland journey to Ontario.

Back at the docks she arrived to a different scene from the day before. The shed was bustling with activity. The fire was blazing and from somewhere a large cauldron had been found to boil water and make soup. The seriously ill were laid out in a row on one side, where they could be fed and tended. On another side women had commandeered the carters' horse troughs for wash tubs. They were beating sea salt out of plaids and blankets, and throwing basins of water into the passage to make a stream for rinsing. The older children had been sent to scavenge round the wharves, while the younger ones had found their land legs and were careering round the neighbouring sheds.

The men were looking out for Flora, and came forward immediately to unload her supplies and stack them carefully in the most sheltered end. As the afternoon's work went on and food was prepared she sat in a circle round the fire listening to the stories and memories. Though there had been some deaths, and sickness was still about, the mood had shifted from despair to hope. Their ship was to sail the next morning. Flora felt sure that the McDonells would settle well in Canada, where land was plentiful and the country by all accounts much like home.

When everyone had eaten, women joined the circle and a first song was put up. Most of this was in Gaelic beyond Flora's recall, but Calum sat close by and kept up a running translation. Then suddenly there was a song that she remembered from her own childhood. It was a song in praise of a great chief of Glen Garry written by a woman bard. Death had felled the highest oak tree in the glen. Flora followed the lines under her breath. He had been the salmon in the river, the soaring eagle in the skies, the stag with antlers wide spread. He was the well of healing, the loch that could not be emptied, the Ben Nevis of every summit, the topmost stone of the castle, the gemstone on a golden ring. He was the yew, the holly and the blackthorn, the apple bough, the blossom and the fruit. He was the last chief of McIvor.

Flora began to feel light headed and made her excuses, promising to return in the morning to wave them off. There were many hugs and bows and hand shakings and blessings, but eventually she got away. By the time she had walked home she felt drained and barely able to move. She dragged herself into bed still in her underskirt. Despite the cold she was thirsty but lacked the energy to get up again for a mug of fresh water.

When Bessie came looking for her early the next morning Flora was running a fever.

'Lorenzo, is that you?'

The old woman dipped a rag in water and mopped her brow.

'Master coming home soon, Missis, Master coming soon to look after you.'

'Thank God. He is coming for me at last.'

Coda

WHEN LORENZO CAME home five days later it was to an empty house. His wife was dead. The doctor had attended her sickbed and prescribed infusions and a liquid diet. But he was unable to contain what he called 'ship's fever'. Trying to make sense of Bessie's garbled account of the Scottish ship and 'famine' relief, Lorenzo went through the required motions. He interred the body in a new cemetery near their home, and attempted to pick up the remaining threads of his life.

As the months wore on he realised how intertwined he and Flora had become since arriving in New York. They had depended on each other more than ever, and he wondered how he might continue. Yet strangely his affairs seemed to flourish without close attention. The Concert Society was established, the University asked him to lecture in Italian literature, and his line in cultured books was increasingly in demand.

One year on, Lorenzo proposed a concert in his wife's memory and the committee gave their sympathetic approval. He had studied Flora's notes on Fionn and Ossian, but was unable to translate them into a musical form. James MacPherson's Ossian would have to prevail for now. Instead he decided on a concert recital of Monteverdi's Orfeo. The committee tactfully suggested the he himself should conduct.

On the night, the University lecture hall in which the society held its events was packed. Such a piece had not been heard before in New York. Because of the personal nature of the occasion, musicians and singers had volunteered to support their city's cultured Italian in his personal tribute.

Lorenzo walked to the lectern and called the performance into being. The underlying mood was brooding, but ornamented with forced happiness as Eurydice appeared. Soon tragic events were unfolding with the venomous sting of a snake the removal of the young queen into the kingdom of death. Orpheus was left bereft as the music moved from disaster to lament. He could not stay in the palace alone, but taking his harp set out in search of his lost love. The scene was transformed by the sounds of lonely woods, where he sat down on a rock and began to sing.

> O doleful harp, with many a string,
> Turn all thy mirth and music into mourning
> And cease from all thy sweet melodies
> To weep with me thy lord and king,
> For I have lost in earth all my Joy –
> Where hast thou gone my Eurydice?

Flutes became birds singing in sad harmony, while the strings trembled like leaves in sympathy.

Orpheus rose from his rock and continued to search, begging the gods to aid his quest. Till suddenly a triple masked monster burst out, courtesy of the percussion – Cerberus, the dread porter, guardian of hell's gate. But Orpheus took up his harp again and lulled the three heads to sleep.

Something menacing entered the music, as a procession of underworld beings encircled Orpheus in a slow dance. They touched him with black wands and nodding dark plumed helmets while he stood bewildered by this phantasmagoria, until Hades and Persephone appeared on two thrones, etched in ebony and silver.

Orpheus went down on one knee, resting his harp on the other, and began to play. This music pled his sorrow and his desire. Persephone turned towards her lord, but he listened impassively until the music faded to its end, when he lifted his right hand and gestured towards the wings. Unnoticed as the music played, Eurydice had stepped into the shadows. Orpheus moved instinctively in her direction but then froze in shock as Eurydice came into the light. His anguish was audible.

> My lovely lady, my delight,
> How are you changed, how –
> Where are your rosy cheeks,
> Your crystal eyes and lashes dark,
> Your lips so red, soft to kiss?

Persephone put a hand on Hades' arm, speaking in a full contralto.

> Lord Hades, king of all below,
> Recall my coming here to dwell,
> My wasting and decline,
> My mother's grief and woe,
> Till your heart gave way
> Yielding the boon of my return.

It seemed at first as if Hades would not even acknowledge this plea, staring inflexibly ahead through the eye slits of his mask. But then the orchestra took up compassion's cause.

Lorenzo felt now that the music was drawing Eurydice out of the underworld. He was walking ahead guiding his love towards the light. And she was following with unfaltering steps. But something – what was it? – the tug of earlier loves, a shadow of the past – halted her progress.

Had she ever been wholly his, or he hers? For an instant she seemed to balance on a delicate foot between two worlds. Then she looked back. Her figure faded into the gloom, pale face dissolving.

But Lorenzo held on, allowing a lament to rise, swelling from strings and wind. Somehow this season of loss was not the final word. He reached out his arms towards her absence. The musicians held their notes keeping faith. Eventually almost beyond belief, Lorenzo's arms fell to his side.

There was an awed silence and then the hall rose as one in ecstatic applause. It was a triumph.

Some other books published by **LUATH PRESS**

The English Spy

Donald Smith

ISBN 1 905222 82 3 PBK £8.99

He was a spy among us, but not known as such, otherwise the mob of Edinburgh would pull him to pieces.
JOHN CLERK OF PENICUIK

Union between England and Scotland hangs in the balance.
Propagandist, spy and novelist-to-be Daniel Defoe is caught up in the murky essence of eighteenth-century Edinburgh – cobblestones, courtesans and kirkyards. Expecting a godly society in the capital of Presbyterianism, Defoe engages with a beautiful Jacobite agent, and uncovers a nest of vipers.

Subtly crafted… and a rattling good yarn. STEWART CONN

Delves into the City of Literature, and comes out dark side up.
MARC LAMBERT

Anyone interested in the months that saw the birth of modern Britain should enjoy this book. THE SUNDAY HERALD

Excellent… a brisk narrative and a vivid sense of time and place.
THE HERALD

Ballad of the Five Marys

Donald Smith

ISBN 978 1 908373 89 2 PBK £8.99

Who was Mary, Queen of Scots? Vilified as an adulteress, only to be immortalised as a martyr; where does history become legend?

Smith's powerful prose ballad gives an intimate and revealing portrait of the enigmatic woman at the centre of the myths, as well as of those who shaped her rule and legacy. The Mary Carmichael of the Ballad of the Five Marys is a fiction, but Marys Seton, Beaton, Livingston and Fleming, together with Mary Stewart, comprised the five Marys, assertive young women unafraid to question their place in society.

Why was Mary deposed? Who killed Darnley? Five hundred years after the Battle of Flodden and birth of John Knox, this new take on Mary's life explores not only the historical events which led to her demise, but the relationships and emotions of an increasingly isolated young woman faced with political and religious upheaval and her country's gradual loss of independence.

Calton Hill: Journeys and Evocations

Stuart McHardy and Donald Smith

ISBN: 978-1-908373-85-4 PBK £7.99

Experience the scenery and folklore of Edinburgh's iconic Calton Hill through new eyes in the second instalment in the Journeys and Evocations series. This blend of prose, poetry, photography and history is the perfect gift for any visitor to Scotland's capital city.

McHardy is driven by a passion for making connections. His vision is of an interconnected, inter-related environment. His values are those of a cultural ecologist, storyteller as well as researcher, poet as well as scholar. He sets out to illuminate and to persuade.
CENCRASTUS

Edinburgh Old Town: Journeys and Evocations

John Fee with Stuart McHardy and Donald Smith

ISBN 978-1-910021-56-9 PBK £7.99

John Fee was a true storytelling artist, painting verbal pictures, setting off on digressions that turned out not to be digressions, moving effortlessly into a song or poem. He has uncovered little-known aspects of the Royal Mile along with long-forgotten characters who spring back to life through the storyteller's art.

Following on from the acclaimed *Arthur's Seat* and *Calton Hill* volumes, this third instalment in the Journeys and Evocations series focuses on the extensive history and folklore surrounding Edinburgh's atmospheric Old Town. Take a vivid trip with John Fee through Edinburgh's Old Town as you've never seen it before, with this wonderful blend of prose, poetry, photography and incredible stories from another era of one of Edinburgh's most renowned districts.

Arthur's Seat: Journeys and Evocations

Stuart McHardy and Donald Smith

ISBN 978-1-908373-46-5 PBK £7.99

Arthur's Seat, rising high above the Edinburgh skyline, is the city's most awe-inspiring landmark. Although thousands climb to the summit every year, its history remains a mystery, shrouded in myth and legend.

The first book of its kind, *Arthur's Seat: Journeys and Evocations* is a salute to the ancient tradition of storytelling, guiding the reader around Edinburgh's famous 'Resting Giant' with an exploration of the local folklore and customs associated with the mountain-within-a-city.

Inspired by NVA's Speed of Light, a major event in Edinburgh's International Festival and the country-wide Cultural Olympiad, this book brings together past and future in a perspective of the Edinburgh landscape like no other.

Two of the city's leading storytellers have sifted through the centuries to compile this remarkable guide to Edinburgh's famous landmarks.
EDINBURGH EVENING NEWS

Death of a Chief

Douglas Watt

ISBN 978-1-906817-31-2 PBK £6.99

The year is 1686. Sir Lachlan MacLean, chief of a proud but poverty-stricken Highland clan, has met with a macabre death in his Edinburgh lodgings. With a history of bad debts, family quarrels, and some very shady associates, Sir Lachlan had many enemies. But while motives are not hard to find, evidence is another thing entirely. It falls to lawyer John MacKenzie and his scribe Davie Scougall to investigate the mystery surrounding the death of the chief, but among the endless possibilities, can Reason prevail in a time of witchcraft, superstition and religious turmoil?

This thrilling tale of suspense plays out against a wonderfully realised backdrop of pre-Enlightenment Scotland, a country on the brink of financial ruin, ruled from London, a country divided politically by religion and geography. The first in the series featuring investigative advocate John MacKenzie, Death of a Chief comes from a time long before police detectives existed.

Sir Walter Scott's Waverley: Newly Adapted for the Modern Reader

Jenni Calder

ISBN 978-1-91002I-25-5 PBK £9.99

Scotland, 1745: Edward Waverley is a naïve English soldier drawn into the heart of the Jacobite rebellion. Charmed by clan leader Fergus MacIvor and his sister Flora, he allies himself with the Jacobite cause – a bold and dangerous move. He finds himself caught between two women – feisty Flora and demure Rose – proving that love can be just as powerful as politics.

First published in 1814, *Waverley* is widely regarded as the first historical novel in the western tradition. This new edition celebrates the 200th anniversary of its publication, and has been expertly reworked for modern readers by Jenni Calder.

Walter Scott has no business to write novels, especially good ones. It is not fair. He has Fame and Profit enough as a Poet, and should not be taking the bread out of other people's mouths. I do not like him, and do not mean to like Waverley *if I can help it – but fear I must.* JANE AUSTEN

The best book by Sir Walter Scott. GOETHE

Sir Walter Scott's The Heart of Midlothian: Newly Adapted for the Modern Reader

David Purdie

ISBN 978-1-908373-90-9 PBK £9.99

Edinburgh, 1736: an indignant crowd has gathered in the Grassmarket to watch the execution of a smuggler. Opening with the start of the Porteous Riots, *The Heart of Midlothian* is one of Walter Scott's most famous historical novels, featuring murder, madness and seduction.

Following his brutal suppression of the spectators, John Porteous, Captain of the Guard, is charged with murder and locked up in Edinburgh's Tolbooth prison, also known as the Heart of Midlothian. When news comes that he has been pardoned, an angry mob breaks into the jail, liberating its inmates and bringing Porteous to its own form of justice. But one prisoner who fails to take this opportunity to flee is Effie Deans, who, wrongly convicted of infanticide, has been sentenced to death. Jeanie, her older sister, sets off to London on foot to beg for her pardon from the queen.

This edition of *The Heart of Midlothian* has been expertly reworked for modern audiences by David Purdie.

Sir Walter Scott's Ivanhoe: Newly Adapted for the Modern Reader
David Purdie
ISBN 978-1-908373-26-7 PBK £9.99

'Fight on, brave knights. Man dies, but glory lives!'

Ivanhoe has been cut down to size in this modern retelling of Scott's classic novel: the original text has been slashed from an epic 194,000 words to a more manageable 95,000.
Banished from his father's court, Wilfred of Ivanhoe returns from Richard the Lionheart's Crusades to claim love, justice and glory. Tyrannical Norman knights, indolent Saxon nobles and the usurper Prince John stand in his way. A saga of tournaments and melees, chivalry and love, nobility and merry men, Ivanhoe's own quest soon becomes a battle for the English throne itself...

This is exactly what's needed in order to rescue Sir Walter Scott.
ALEXANDER MCCALL SMITH

Knights getting shorter... [Ivanhoe] has been brought up to date by Professor David Purdie who is president of the Sir Walter Scott Society and should know the ropes. THE HERALD

Testament of a Witch
Douglas Watt
ISBN 978-1-908373-21-2 PBK £7.99

I confess that I am a witch. I have sold myself body and soul unto Satan. My mother took me to the Blinkbonny Woods where we met other witches. I put a hand on the crown of my head and the other on the sole of my foot. I gave everything between unto him.

Scotland, late 17th century. A young woman is accused of witchcraft. Tortured with pins and sleep deprivation, she is using all of her strength to resist confessing...

During the Scottish witch-hunt around 1,000 men and women were executed for witchcraft before the frenzy died down.

When Edinburgh-based Advocate John MacKenzie and his assistant Davie Scougall investigate the suspicious death of a woman denounced as a witch, they find themselves in a village overwhelmed by superstition, resentment and puritanical religion. In a time of spiritual, political and social upheaval, will reason allow MacKenzie to reveal the true evil lurking in the town, before the witch-hunt claims yet another victim?

Details of these and other books published by Luath Press can be found at:
www.luath.co.uk

Luath Press Limited
committed to publishing well written books worth reading

LUATH PRESS takes its name from Robert Burns, whose little collie Luath (*Gael.*, swift or nimble) tripped up Jean Armour at a wedding and gave him the chance to speak to the woman who was to be his wife and the abiding love of his life. Burns called one of 'The Twa Dogs' Luath after Cuchullin's hunting dog in Ossian's *Fingal*. Luath Press was established in 1981 in the heart of Burns country, and is now based a few steps up the road from Burns' first lodgings on Edinburgh's Royal Mile.

Luath offers you distinctive writing with a hint of unexpected pleasures.

Most bookshops in the UK, the US, Canada, Australia, New Zealand and parts of Europe either carry our books in stock or can order them for you. To order direct from us, please send a £sterling cheque, postal order, international money order or your credit card details (number, address of cardholder and expiry date) to us at the address below. Please add post and packing as follows: UK – £1.00 per delivery address; overseas surface mail – £2.50 per delivery address; overseas airmail – £3.50 for the first book to each delivery address, plus £1.00 for each additional book by airmail to the same address. If your order is a gift, we will happily enclose your card or message at no extra charge.

Luath Press Limited
543/2 Castlehill
The Royal Mile
Edinburgh EH1 2ND
Scotland
Telephone: 0131 225 4326 (24 hours)
Fax: 0131 225 4324
email: sales@luath.co.uk
Website: www.luath.co.uk